SUGAR ALPHA

SUGAR DADDIES #12

CHARITY PARKERSON

Sugar Alpha
Sugar Daddies #12
Charity Parkerson

--Warning: This book is intended for readers over the age of 18.

Editor: BZ Hercules & Consultants
ISBN: 978-1-946099-48-8

❀ Created with Vellum

INTRODUCTION

Since losing his husband, Flynn has been waiting for a sign his life hasn't stopped. He's about to get one.

It's been a few years since Flynn's husband passed away. Since losing the love of his life, he's been stuck in traction. He's good at being a dom. Working at the Den of Payne keeps him busy. It's not sexual. He doesn't need the money. The job simply fills his empty days. Flynn is convinced his heart no longer works, and then he meets Jake.

Jake hates his life. Everything about it. Every day when he walks into work, he dreams of quitting and running away from his family's expectations. The weight of being the perfect son, brother, and lawyer is crushing him. Jake can't see a way out. Right when Jake thinks he'll suffocate, Flynn pushes his way into Jake's life. Flynn is controlling and dominant. He's also loving and everything Jake never knew he needed.

Flynn's refusal to allow Jake to disobey might just be the thing that finally sets Jake free. It's possible becoming Jake's daddy is what Flynn's been preparing for his whole life too.

ONE

THEY WERE GOING on two hours. Even though it wasn't unusual for Jake's parents to drag out a lecture for as long as possible, it was like they'd created notecards for this one. Jake's dad had moved on to bargaining ten minutes ago. As he outlined a plan to pay Jake's bills for six months if he passed his bar exam, Jake's mind wandered. An image of Flynn filled his head as he'd been the night they'd met. They'd been attending Brad and Kato's engagement party. Flynn insisted Jake drink champagne with him in private. Since Jake was there because his employer had demanded it, he'd been good with slipping away. If he'd only known...

Flynn tossed back the last of his champagne.

Jake's gaze locked on the way his throat moved as he swallowed. It had been several months since anyone had caught Jake's eye. Thanks to his mom's campaign for governor, he didn't go anywhere he might meet someone his type. He preferred earthy men. Someone not afraid to get dirty. Everything about Flynn screamed he would fuck Jake hard and disappoint Jake's parents with his existence. Jake's mouth was dry.

Flynn set his champagne flute aside. His sexy blue gaze landed on Jake. He gave his knee a pat. "You should come sit in Daddy's lap. You won't need your pants."

A party still raged outside the door of the private room inside the Den of Payne. It was his first time inside the exclusive sex club. He never would've expected he'd find himself in this predicament. "I've known you less than two hours. For now, I think I'd like to hang on to my pants."

"No."

Jake's lips twitched at the memory. Flynn's bossy tone always made him hot.

"Do you think this is funny? Your mother and I paid a fortune for your education, only to have you waste your life working as a paralegal." His dad said

2

"paralegal" in the same way most people spoke of dog shit.

"Being part of the legal team at Green's Fighter Fuel looks good on a resume."

His mom and dad snorted in unison. They flashed each other a smile and air kissed.

Jake went back to his happy place where he kept his nights with Flynn.

"I don't kiss."

Funny. Jake hadn't even noticed the lack. "Okay."

"I don't want you to get the wrong idea about us."

Same. Jake wouldn't get to keep Flynn. Sooner or later, Jake would have to go back to living for his family. He'd have to pretend he was someone else twenty-four seven. "I don't expect more."

An odd look passed over Flynn's features. Flynn shook his head as if trying to expel his thoughts. "Tell me something about you no one else knows."

"You don't want to know me." Even Jake heard the unhappiness in his confession.

Flynn's arms tightened around him. His lips brushed the shell of Jake's ear. "Maybe you don't know yourself."

That was true and maybe it was better that way. If Jake dared to have hopes and dreams, then he'd see how much he lost every day when he followed his family's plan for him. "On the bright side, that means I can be whoever you want," *Jake said, trying to move away from telling Flynn anything personal.* "What's your fantasy?"

A contented sigh rose in Jake's throat as Flynn's fingers ran through his hair and massaged his scalp. "The only fantasy I have right now is you." *Something shifted in Jake's chest. He couldn't look away from Flynn's sexy light blue stare. Flynn's lips curved into a wicked smile.* "On your knees, brat."

"Do we have a deal?"

At his father's question, Jake was ripped from his memories. He blinked, wondering what he'd missed. Not that it mattered. He'd agree to anything to make this end. "Of course." It wasn't as if he had a choice anyhow.

His response was met with matching smiles of pride. "Excellent," his mother said, sounding too much like the cat who'd killed the canary. "I'll call Craig on Monday and let him know you'll be joining his firm in the near future."

Jake blinked. Fuck. What had he agreed to while dreaming? He walked to his car in a haze. How had this happened? He couldn't breathe. Jake drove. There was no destination mapped out inside his head. He just wanted freedom. Invisible chains draped him, weighing down his soul. He loved his family, but he also thought he maybe hated them too. Most people were allowed to grow up and move on. Not Jake. Not only had he been expected to act like an adult his entire life, he was also expected to continue obeying as a child would. He was exhausted. Jake wanted to drive and drive until he reached the edge of the earth. Then he wanted to keep going until this world no longer mattered.

He came back to reality. Jake realized he'd been sitting in the parking lot of the Den of Payne for several minutes. He didn't recall a single moment of the drive. Much less did he understand why he'd come here. An image of Flynn floated through his mind. Jake's eyes fell closed. The tension seeped from his shoulders. He took a breath. Jake didn't have a membership. He wouldn't go inside, but Flynn was here. Jake swore he could feel him. A loud knock on his window sent his heart racing into his throat. His eyes flew open. A large blond man with hard features and sensual eyes stood on the other side. Jake rolled down the window.

The guy didn't bother with pleasantries. "Come on. Flynn isn't busy right now."

Jake shook his head. Horror had blood rushing to his face. The man looked somewhat familiar, but he was certain they hadn't met. "It's okay. I don't have a membership."

A blinding smile lit the man's face. "I'm Payne. If I say it's cool, you're good. Come on."

Jake's stomach tied into knots. He pushed the button, rolling up his window and killed the ignition. If ever he'd thought he was making a huge mistake, this was the time. Flynn didn't know he was coming. There was no reason for Jake to be here. He felt like a fucking idiot, seeking out the most popular dom at a well-known BDSM club—like a fucking crazed stalker. Still, he followed on Payne's heels to the door. Jake kept his head down. After passing through the front door, Jake didn't look left or right. He shouldn't be here, and he knew it. Flynn would probably think he was pathetic and needy—like he already did with Jake's brother. In his defense, Jake hadn't meant to come here. It was just something stupid—like his heart, leading him. Ugh. He was ridiculous.

"He's in room ten. Just head inside."

Jake fought the urge to run away. Instead, he mumbled his thanks and scurried down the hall while wishing the floor would swallow him whole. He couldn't recall the last time he'd been this horrified.

At door ten, Jake didn't pause. He was scared he would chicken out if he did. The moment the door inched open, Flynn turned his way. Everything inside Jake went silent. Visually, Flynn was amazing. He was beautiful in a way few people achieved. God had made that. That was the only explanation for how flawless he was from his perfectly shaped eyebrows to his sleek muscles. Light blue eyes and tall frame. Today, he wore a kilt and boots. His chest was bare. When the light caught his hair, Jake could see that the dark locks were actually more red than brown. But on the inside, Flynn was even more gorgeous. He was blinding. Jake had never meet anyone else so in tune with the world around him. He fixed people in ways Jake could only dream. Not everyone had what he did.

"Jake."

Goddamn. The way Jake's name rolled off Flynn's tongue in that Scottish brogue was enough to weaken his knees. "Hi. Payne let me in." Jake shook his head. "Actually, he kind of made me come in here."

Flynn's gaze moved over Jake's features. "What's wrong?"

Jake's shoulders lifted. Even he didn't know. Everything was wrong.

Without a word, Flynn crossed the room. Jake stood frozen with his hand still wrapped around the doorknob. He fought the impulse to flee. Flynn pried his fingers away from the knob. "You should probably stand on the other side of this." He urged Jake inside and closed the door, shutting out the world. There was next to nothing inside the room other than two stools, a hook hanging from the ceiling, and two suitcases Jake knew from experience held Flynn's gear. Flynn led him to one of the stools. "Sit."

Jake sat.

Flynn moved to the other stool. Once settled, with the heels of his boots perched on the rungs of the stool, he eyed Jake. Jake stared back, transfixed by the vision he presented. "Tell me."

It was odd. No one else could pull so much from Jake with so few words. But Jake thought it likely no one else saw him either. Not really. "I just sat through a two-hour lecture about how I've been a paralegal long enough and it's time for me to get my shit in line to practice law as ordered. Pass the bar exam. Stop being an overall failure. That sort of thing." Jake still couldn't explain why he'd come here. Honestly, he hadn't thought at all. The pains in his chest had sent him straight to Flynn. He couldn't breathe beneath the expectations.

"Explain."

It was funny how the bite to Flynn's voice and the anger flashing in his eyes loosened the grip on Jake's lungs. He was safe here. Free. "My mom is running for governor. She has two gay sons." Jake knew that wasn't much of an explanation, but then again, it was everything. "One is one thing. Having one gay son is reaching a certain demographic, but two..." Jake shook his head.

Flynn leaned forward. The muscles from his wrists to his shoulders flexed as he repositioned the stool beneath him. Jake didn't think it had been a purposeful move, but his gaze still moved immediately to enjoy the show. Flynn's sexy gaze never wavered from Jake. Of course, Flynn's single-minded intensity was one of the qualities Jake couldn't resist. His accent was another. "You know, statistics show if you have one gay child, there's about an eighty percent chance you'll have two. So, truthfully, they shouldn't be surprised."

"I don't think they were," Jake said honestly. "I also don't think they care. However, they do care that at least one of their sons follow in their footsteps. They want at least one lawyer and at least one son married with children. I mean, it's not that big of a deal if Easton plays around, doing as he pleases, as long as he is doing so on the arm of someone successful. Unfortunately, that leaves me as the one they're hinging their expectations." This was why he'd ended up here. He could say anything. Flynn would listen. Somehow, he'd known that without even thinking.

"What would happen if you stopped living for them?"

The absurdity of the idea had a smile snapping to Jake's lips. He stood and crossed the room. Jake couldn't resist another second. His heart beat a little faster with every step. Flynn looked curious and expectant as if he waited to see what Jake would do. Jake didn't think. The moment his hands landed on Flynn's bare shoulders, he caressed. His palms slid up Flynn's shoulders until they met at Flynn's nape. He linked his fingers and held on. Flynn dropped one booted foot to the floor, making room for Jake to stand between his spread knees. His kilt slid higher on his raised knee as his hands slipped across Jake's waist and urged Jake closer.

Jake couldn't explain his actions. He just needed Flynn. "What do you suggest? Should I quit my job at Green's and stop working toward practicing law?"

Flynn's intense light blue stare never wavered. "Yes."

Jake couldn't stop. "I suppose I should take up with some guy who spanks people for a living and is notoriously shameless. Oh, and never, ever speak to my spoiled brother again."

"You should definitely do all of that."

Jake's smile slipped away. His throat swelled. Until the words were out there, he'd never realized how badly he wanted that freedom. "If only I was that brave." Jake's voice came out in a whisper. Most people would be thrilled with the success he'd achieved. Jake hated it. He despised everything about the life not of his choosing that suffocated him. Being with Flynn was the only rebellion he'd allowed himself in forever. Sooner or later, he would have to give this up too. The thought of going back to the emptiness he'd lived in before Flynn choked him. Flynn wasn't his, but he felt like it when they were together. When they were apart, Jake knew Flynn spent the rest of his time entertaining other men. Jake was just another face. Another body. But that was how desperate Jake was for anything that made him feel real; he didn't care. He swallowed past the lump forming in his throat. Right now, they were alone. In this moment, with Flynn focused completely on him, those other men didn't exist. A spark of courage raced through Jake. Before he could change his mind, he pressed his lips to Flynn's. His bravado fled the moment their lips met. Jake pulled away. He kept his gaze averted.

"Sorry." He shook his head. "I shouldn't have..." Helplessness overcame him. He always made the worst decisions. "You probably have a full schedule. I should go." Without looking Flynn's way, he tried stepping out of Flynn's hold. Flynn's arms tightened around him. Jake's gaze snapped to Flynn's without thought. Flynn's stare held him captive. It hurt. He'd never wanted anyone for himself as badly as Jake wished Flynn was his. Jake wasn't Flynn's client, but he also wasn't Flynn's man. They were... nothing.

"I didn't give you permission to leave."

Jake held still, waiting. Flynn didn't say anything else, but he still didn't tell Jake to go. An uncomfortably long moment passed before Jake realized Flynn didn't intend to say more. The silence between them deepened. Without thought, Jake's gaze dropped to Flynn's lips again. They were made for sin. This time, it had nothing to do with courage. It was need. Jake was one hundred percent certain he'd die if he didn't kiss Flynn. Of all the times in his life he thought he might suffocate beneath the weight of his life, nothing compared to staring at Flynn's lips and longing. He was drowning without Flynn's kiss. Flynn was the only life preserver in an ocean of bullshit. This time, Jake didn't pull away when their lips met. Flynn's hands moved from Jake's back to his ass. He hauled Jake closer. Jake went willingly. There was so much skill in Flynn's kiss, Jake swore he felt the man's brogue in the stroke of his tongue. The immediate lust was crippling. Flynn led Jake's hand to his thigh. The moment Flynn's hot skin touched his palm, Jake moaned. Flynn urged Jake to push his kilt higher, giving him permission to touch Flynn the way he always wanted.

"Do you want me, baby boy?"

Jake couldn't lie. He also couldn't hide the way his erection strained against his pants. "Yes." Even to his ears he sounded desperate with his lips still brushing Flynn's every chance they could.

"Then be a good boy and tell me the dream you had for yourself before someone else chose your future."

Jake leaned away and blinked. The spell Flynn wove lost some of its hold. He shook his head. A smile that felt faked, even to him, stretched his lips. "Forget I said anything. There's nothing wrong with the life I have. Anyone would be thrilled to be part of Jude and John Green's legal team."

Flynn's expression snapped closed. He gently nudged Jake away and stood. "You're right. I have a full schedule. You should go. Also, don't ever kiss me again without my permission."

A knot formed in Jake's gut. Even though he hadn't raised his voice, it was obvious Flynn was angry with him, or disappointed, or worse—both. His throat swelled. No one else had ever seen him so clearly. Even though he wasn't sure what they were to each other, Jake didn't want to lose this. Not yet. No one else set him free.

"It's stupid. I thought, for a little while in college, that I might like to open a bookstore. Personally, I think all these stores that rent textbooks to college students are price gouging." Jake cringed as he made the confession. He could already hear his mother's disapproving sigh and his father's laughter. E-readers were the future. No one bought books anymore, especially from independent sellers. Even the major chains were on the edge of bankruptcy. A self-deprecating smile tugged at Jake's lips. He shook his head. "It was a ridiculous idea, though."

Jake found his space suddenly crowded. Flynn's bare chest collided with Jake. Without

14

warning, a solid and painful slap landed on his ass. "That was for calling your dreams stupid." Jake couldn't breathe. Flynn smoothed his hand over the spot on Jake's ass that stung. "Don't ever hide your thoughts from me. You're allowed to want something for yourself, because you want it, and it's your life. No one else has to live inside your head, listening to the screams." Flynn's gaze remained hard—like Jake still wasn't forgiven. He stroked Jake's jaw. "Now tell me you're sorry for trying to lie to me."

"I wasn't—"

Another slap—just as hard as the last—landed across Jake's ass. "Who do you think you're talking to right now?"

Jake was nearly crippled by lust. Goddamn. Flynn was everything he needed. "I'm sorry, Flynn."

Flynn's hard edge didn't soften. "Did I tell you that you could use my name? Baby boys who lie don't get to use my name."

There was barely enough blood making the trip to Jake's brain for him to think. "I'm sorry, Daddy."

"Did you come here so I could make you feel better?"

He'd already gotten in trouble for lying. "Yes."

Flynn's hand slid down Jake's body, stopping at

his belt. "What did you think I would do to make you better?"

Jake couldn't look away from Flynn's expression. He looked focused—like no one else existed. "I didn't expect you'd do a thing. All I wanted was to see your face."

Flynn blinked, as if taken aback.

Jake looked away. "I've done that, so I guess I should go."

Flynn touched Jake's jaw. Jake immediately leaned into his touch. The move had his gaze colliding with Flynn's once more. He saw something he couldn't describe in Flynn's stare. Then Flynn kissed him. The air left Jake's lungs in a rush, making him lightheaded. Their lips brushed, sweetly tasting. Flynn shuffled closer. His mouth opened over Jake's. His intensity forced Jake's head back beneath the onslaught. He was at Flynn's mercy as always. There was a lot going on inside Jake's chest. Flynn had made it clear he didn't kiss anyone—ever. Not only had Flynn sought him out as a sexual partner, something else he also rarely did, Flynn constantly broke his self-imposed rules for Jake. It was worth puzzling over. Jake couldn't stop touching him, memorizing the contours of Flynn's every rib and the curve of his spine. Maybe this would be the last time

Flynn broke his rules and kissed Jake. Jake needed every detail to commit to memory. He planned to relive this every chance he got. Flynn's kiss softened. His touch turned sweet. He caressed Jake with such care that Jake's eyes stung. Jake wanted to be special. It was stupid. Flynn was who he was. Jake couldn't change that nor did he care to reshape Flynn into some perfect boyfriend image. Flynn mattered. He gave people peace. People like Jake. But Jake's ridiculous heart still craved like a blind fool. That idiotic muscle didn't know Flynn couldn't be tamed. It just wanted to be loved.

"Are you better?" Flynn asked between kisses. "Did I fix you for now?"

Jake pulled away and dropped his forehead to Flynn's chest. For a moment, he stared down at the space between them. He already felt the loss of Flynn. "Yes." Maybe he was lying again. Jake couldn't tell.

"Baby boy."

At Flynn's sweet tone, Jake lifted his chin. "Yes, Daddy."

"You don't need this place. Don't come back here."

A lump formed in Jake's throat, choking him. "Okay." Even to his ears, Jake sounded broken.

"Don't do that, baby boy. That's not what I meant. You can still call me or text me anytime. I'll happily see you outside this place, but there's nothing for you here. What you need isn't under this roof."

He was wrong, but Jake didn't argue. He nodded. His voice no longer worked. Jake felt his only lifeline slipping away. He wasn't ready to lose the only person who saw the real him.

"Go home. Take a shower and relax. Get that hole lubed and prepped. Put a few condoms on the coffee table and wait for me. I'll come to you."

The tightness eased in Jake's chest. Flynn would come to him. Even if it was for the last time, Jake needed one more night with Flynn. Tomorrow. He would do better tomorrow.

IT TOOK FLYNN LESS THAN AN HOUR TO TAKE care of business. He rushed a little more than he cared to admit. Three months ago, when he met Jake, he'd only meant the man to be a night's worth of distraction. Then Jake had forced him to work to get him out of his pants and onto his lap, and then out of his underwear. Basically, he'd been reduced to damn near begging for Jake's attention. Jake had made it crystal clear he didn't need Flynn. He could find pleasure on his own. Flynn used every ounce of skill and brainpower each time they were together, trying to figure out how to bend Jake to his will. It was funny how three solid months of working to crush Jake's walls had broken Flynn down instead, making him wonder sometimes which of them was truly in charge.

Flynn tried keeping his mind blank on the drive to Jake's. He was torn. On one hand, Flynn wanted to make Jake's entire family pay for the corner they kept Jake backed into. On the other, Jake's family had shaped Jake into the person he was. If Jake didn't come off as an abrasive snob to everyone else, then someone would've claimed the man long before they'd met. Jake possessed a polished veneer that only an expensive education and a lifetime of high living could create. It was a facade. Inside, Jake was love starved, awkward, and screaming for help. He was gorgeous in an unapproachable way with his perfectly styled brown hair and cutting green eyes. When Flynn set him free, Jake was sexy to the point he stole Flynn's breath and made him weak. Flynn readjusted himself as his dick stirred. Just the thought of the way Jake came unglued in Flynn's arms had Flynn ready to fuck. He needed to find his control. Jake needed Flynn to wash away the day. Flynn had to consider all options. Find his footing.

Jake's townhouse came into view. Flynn slowed. He parked his older model Chevy Suburban in the empty parking spot at Jake's assigned garage. Flynn didn't jump out and rush to the door the way his mind screamed for him to do. Instead, he stared at the white and brick three-story building and took a few calming breaths. His heart raced at the idea of being with Jake. He needed to get that reaction under control and don an unaffected mask. Jake cared about him. Flynn knew that much. But Jake could still live without him. Flynn hadn't completely won him yet. Flynn wanted to own him in every way. Jake's polished veneer hid a kink. Inside, Jake was twisted and dirty. Ready to play in the muck with Flynn. They were more alike than Jake knew. Unlike Flynn's clients, who came to Flynn for relief from the daily grind, Jake sank to Flynn's level because he couldn't stop his deep-seeded desires once his walls fell. In the throes of passion, his true colors showed. He was beautiful in Flynn's eyes. Flynn had seen the real him from the very beginning...

On his knees with his lips swollen from biting them, Jake stared up at Flynn with unfocused eyes and open need. He wouldn't break and beg. Flynn feared he might be the one who pled for more. He dropped to one knee and got on Jake's level. Flynn held Jake's chin, ensuring he couldn't turn his head. He moved slow. Need set his skin on fire. His lips tingled with a desire he'd thought died with William. His lips barely brushed Jake's, and the fire blazed into an inferno. Jake jerked back as if he felt the heat.

"You said you don't kiss anyone."

It hadn't been a lie. Flynn hadn't kissed a soul since William left him alone in the world. "You're not anyone," Flynn explained before capturing Jake's lips. This time, Jake let it happen. He fought like a wildcat to get closer to Flynn. His short nails scratched and bit into Flynn's skin as Jake tried climbing Flynn. Flynn fell backward, bringing Jake with him. Jake never broke their kiss. In his usual shy and awkward state, Jake would never make the first move, but it seemed—if Flynn gave him license—Jake would rip the skin from Flynn's body to be an inch closer. His taste... goddamn. Flynn was lost.

Flynn opened his truck door and slipped out. His hunger hardened his features as he shut his door and headed for Jake's. His knuckles barely brushed the wood before Jake stood in its place, wearing only a towel around his waist. Flynn eyed Jake's body as he stepped inside. He was sleek and tight. Youth made him glow. With his hair slicked back from his shower, Jake looked even younger than his twenty-six years. Flynn's stare never wavered. Jake stepped back as Flynn walked forward. He kicked the door closed behind him as he snagged Jake's waist and hauled him forward. Flynn snatched the towel and ripped it away. He'd let his thoughts carry him away. Now his patience was gone. Jake was about to get fucked— hard and painful. He palmed Jake's erection and massaged. Jake held on to Flynn's shoulders. His eyes fell closed. At Flynn's urging, he spread his stance, making room for Flynn to finger his asshole.

"Good boy. You did as I said." His gaze moved to the cherry wood coffee table. Condoms and lube waited. Flynn's lust hit a new high. His gaze slid back Jake's way. Jake chewed his bottom lip, looking worried, and making Flynn wonder how he looked while starved for Jake's body. "Kiss me." Jake's open nervousness appeared to double at the order. Flynn softened his tone. "What I said earlier about not kissing me without my permission—forget that. I was mad because you weren't being real with me. Your kisses are mine. Only mine. Kiss me."

Jake shuffled closer. His gaze dropped to Flynn's mouth. Flynn's stomach growled. His skin tightened.

Then Jake's lips touched his. Flynn exploded into action. He ripped Jake from his feet and headed for the couch. In a move that was no more than a blur to Flynn's desire-soaked brain, he had Jake face down and ass up, bent over the couch in a flash. His hands shook as he freed his cock and ripped into a condom. It took longer than his rage could handle, rolling the sheath down his length. This was why he'd ordered Jake to have his ass ready to go. Flynn knew himself around Jake. He didn't have the patience to wait through all the steps. Flynn needed Jake's tight heat sucking him deeper.

He didn't ease up once he buried himself in Jake's ass. If anything, his lust skyrocketed. Flynn grabbed Jake's jaw and hauled him upright where Jake could barely move, and Flynn had all the control. He loosened his knees and set the rhythm. His teeth found Jake's back in several places. The moans coming from Jake's throat and vibrating against Flynn's palm drove Flynn crazy. Jake was already tight. Held in this position, he was damn near crippling Flynn. There was ecstasy in pain. Sometimes it was hard to tell the difference in the two. His free hand collided with Jake's cock. Pre-cum soaked his crown and wet Flynn's hand. Flynn stroked. A hint of madness bled away. He pulled out and spun Jake in his arms. Their mouths found each other. Flynn grabbed two handfuls of ass and lifted, leaving Jake no other choice than to wrap his legs around Flynn's hips. Those long legs. Damn. He made Flynn hot.

Flynn moved to the couch and sat. "Ride my dick, sexy," Flynn ordered as he changed angles and went back to trying to suck Jake's tongue. Jake fumbled to comply with Flynn being willfully unhelpful. He still managed. Flynn sucked in a hiss as Jake took him inside. He needed Jake on this crazed level. Flynn fisted Jake's cock as Jake lifted and lowered, setting the pace. Jake clung to the back of the couch as he balanced his weight on his feet and bounced on Flynn's dick. Flynn beat at Jake's erection fast—like it was his. He moved at a pace Jake couldn't match from his position. All Flynn wanted was cum coating his skin. He fought for air with the friction of Jake's ass pulling at his dick. The sounds of sex, jacking off, and moans reverberated from the walls. Part of Flynn wanted to close his eyes and savor the music they made. The rest of Flynn couldn't look away. Jake looked beautiful on his cock. Flynn would proudly wear him all day. Jake's body hardened. His asshole tightened on Flynn's dick. He threw his head back and cried out as cum slapped

Flynn in the chest and flew into the air. A drop landed on Flynn's bottom lip. He licked it away. The salty treat was exactly what Flynn needed. His entire body stiffened, and his lungs seized. The pleasure pounding at his crown exploded into a blinding ecstasy that stole Flynn's control. His body twitched with no input from Flynn. Flynn squeezed Jake's hips between his hands as he ground deeper into Jake's ass, trying to imprint on his soul. Even once the last wave of pleasure passed, the madness didn't. Flynn needed more. His fingers found Jake's hair, tugging and towing him in for more kisses. Their tongues wiggled against each other in a dance that made Flynn's heart sing. This was his favorite part. The mutual existence on a higher level after the storm was over. These moments when the kisses were an emotion that had nothing to do with lust. These kisses were a special breed. Jake was special.

THE WAY FLYNN HELD HIM AND STARED INTO Jake's eyes... whoa. Jake could barely breathe. Flynn massaged every place he could reach while they sat with their foreheads pressed together. Jake soaked up the attention. Most of the time, he didn't realize how starved for affection he was until Flynn focused on him. Then Jake became the glutton, eating up Flynn's tenderness like he'd been on a diet of solitude for years. Flynn had promised to fix Jake. He'd kept his word. All the ugliness that filled Jake after a two-hour lecture was gone. It was like the time beneath his parents' disappointment happened years ago rather than hours. He wished... Jake tried freezing his thoughts before they accepted a truth that would cripple him. There was no stopping the tidal wave of self-reflection. He wished Flynn loved him. Jake wished they were a real couple and Flynn was his barrier from the ugliness he didn't know how to escape. Jake knew Flynn would stand in front of him and block him from his parents' wrath if he chose to go his own way. He knew if he chose to walk away from his family, Flynn would be there if he belonged to Jake.

A smile tugged at the corners of his mouth. He leaned away and shook his head, dispelling the fantasies of another life.

Flynn buried his fingers in Jake's hair and scrubbed at his scalp. "Tell me what that smile's all about."

Jake's lips stretched wider. With his eyes closed, the sensation of Flynn massaging his head was all that penetrated his euphoria. Not even embarrassment over his wayward thoughts reached him. "An image of my parents meeting you just popped in my head. I was envisioning how that would go."

A sexy chuckle vibrated from Flynn. The fluttering in Jake's chest and stomach increased. "I imagine it would go very poorly." He pulled Jake closer and pressed a sweet kiss to Jake's lips. "But the fact that you'd even think of introducing someone like me to your parents is humbling. I don't rank many introductions."

Flynn's confession left Jake stunned. "I'd be proud to take you anywhere. Even though I don't have friends per se, since I'm socially inept, there's no one I wouldn't be willing for you to meet."

For a long moment, Flynn stared at him in silence. His closed expression gave nothing away. "We should go to dinner," Flynn announced suddenly, as if the idea just occurred to him. With one arm wrapped around Jake's waist, he stood, leaving Jake no other choice but to drop his feet to the floor. Flynn pressed another quick kiss to Jake's lips. "Yes. We should definitely go to dinner, but first, a shower." He linked his fingers through Jake's. Jake followed in a stunned silence. They hadn't gone anywhere together in the past three months. They just sort of fucked and slept in the same bed. Jake had never even been to Flynn's house. In truth, he didn't even know where the man lived. They weren't a couple. Possibly. Hell, he didn't know what they were. But Jake wanted them to be real on a visceral level he couldn't describe. He would do whatever it took to get there.

"Better yet, I'll cook you dinner," Flynn said, taking Jake by surprise. "Would you like to see my house?"

Jake fought his excitement. Flynn was letting him in his life a little more every day. "I'd love to."

Flynn walked backward, holding Jake's hands and leading him toward the bathroom. "Take a shower with me first. Then we'll go."

"Okay." Anything Flynn wanted, it was his.

FLYNN WATCHED JAKE'S REACTION AS THEY headed for his front door. He'd purposely never brought Jake here before. The more time he spent with Jake, the more Flynn gave of himself. Jake didn't realize it, but he'd been deeper in Flynn's life and under his skin than anyone had been in years.

"This is a nice neighborhood," Jake finally said, alleviating some of Flynn's anticipation. "Spanking people has been good to you."

"Aye."

Jake had been raised with money. Flynn didn't doubt for a second, Jake knew there was no way Flynn made enough money working for Payne to afford this house. Jake didn't question him. In fact, he barely glanced at his surroundings as they stepped through the door. His gaze was for Flynn alone. Jake wasn't the type to care about a person's wealth. He craved the things he'd never had—attention, affection, and approval. When it came to Jake, Flynn had no problem offering that triple A service. There was something about being the subject of Jake's intense focus. He made Flynn want to show him everything. Breaking down Jake's wall when no else ever had; that was a fucking power trip like Flynn couldn't describe.

Flynn tossed his keys on the table by the door. "Would you like to see my bedroom?"

Jake nodded.

Flynn craved seeing how far Jake would go. "This way," he said, motioning toward a nearby hallway. Their footsteps sounded loud on the marble hallway floor. Flynn kept glancing Jake's way, waiting for the questions he was sure would come. Jake still didn't look around, as Flynn would've done, passing rooms in a new place. It was obvious Jake wasn't interested in anything inside Flynn's home, except Flynn. Flynn's hunger grew by the second along with some other emotions he refused to acknowledge.

Inside his bedroom, Jake showed his first spark of interest. He glanced in every direction. A smile touched his lips. He shook his head.

Flynn had to know his thoughts. "What's that smile about?"

Jake's laughing gaze landed on Flynn. His smile grew. "It's just a normal bedroom."

At Jake's claim, Flynn looked around. His bed was huge. Flynn had searched for and bought the best bed he could find. All his furniture was real wood and hand carved, and Jake thought it was all ordinary. "Okay."

Jake snorted. "You," he said, motioning toward Flynn. "*The* Dom of the Den of Payne. You have a normal bedroom." A bark of laughter escaped Jake. He covered his mouth, as if trying to hold in his laughter. His eyes shone bright with it, and Flynn could still see his smile. Jake's happiness was the sexiest sight Flynn had ever seen.

"It's not exactly normal," Flynn said, trying to sound mysterious.

Interest lit Jake's eyes. "Really? Tell me more."

Flynn crowded Jake's space. His hands found their way beneath Jake's shirt. "You're here now. That makes this an extraordinary bedroom."

Jake's arms wound around Flynn's neck. His voice turned sultry. "Is that so?"

The air thickened, making it harder to breathe. Jake always had a way of stealing the oxygen from the room. "Yep," Flynn said, answering Jake's question. "This room is also magic."

"Magic?"

Flynn nodded. "Uh-huh. It'll make your clothes disappear."

Jake pulled an adorable face of disbelief. "Are you sure? We're both still fully clothed."

With a few well-placed steps, Flynn maneuvered Jake to the edge of the bed. "I'm verra sure." Flynn's accent thickened. "In fact, I can hear the walls whispering. They say you'll soon be nude and tied to the bed." The interest that lit Jake's eyes had Flynn's mouth watering. It would be a long night. Flynn could already feel it. Jake was more twisted than he knew. Flynn saw it. As their lips met, Flynn accepted the truth—he wouldn't stop. When it came to Jake,

Flynn would dig and push until he'd ripped away every defense and shredded every false puritan pretense. Soon enough, Jake wouldn't remember who he'd been before Flynn. Then, Jake would freely admit who owned him.

TWO

FLYNN: *I'm done for the day. What about you?*

Jake: *I don't get off for another two hours.*

Flynn: *That's a shame. I wanted to be the one to get you off.*

Jake: *That could be arranged. If you want to go my place and wait for me, I'll tell you where you can find the spare key and give you the alarm code.*

Flynn: *That's a lot of trust, baby boy.*

Jake: *I do trust you.*

Flynn: *Good boy. Hit me.*

JAKE: *THEY'RE SENDING EVERYONE HOME EARLY*

today so employees can join the Green family for a grand opening thing. Want to come?

Flynn: *I'd love to come. Text me the address.*

Jake: *That's not what I meant. Meet me at my place.*

Flynn: *I'll be there.*

FLYNN: *I WAS HELPING KATO WITH THE CALENDAR today. He does this thing where we poke pinholes on each day, and he can count them by touch to check the date. Anyhow, we were working on that and I got to thinking. Did you know we've been a couple for six months?*

Jake: *I didn't even realize you considered us a couple.*

Flynn: *I'm going to assume you meant that as a joke, so I'm not forced to punish you.*

Jake: *I don't know. What sort of punishment are we talking here? I mean, I might be down for that.*

Flynn: *Brat.*

JAKE: *YOU LEFT FOR WORK EARLY THIS MORNING. I didn't get to say goodbye.*

Flynn: *Sorry. I had a client who needed an early appointment.*

Jake: *That's fine. It just feels like everything is out of whack today since I didn't get to kiss you before you left.*

Flynn: *It won't happen again. From now on, I'll wake you before I leave.*

Jake: *Okay.*

HIS POSITION AT GREEN'S FIGHTER FUEL WAS usually a quiet one. Since Jake wasn't good at making friends, he tended to keep to himself. Still, today, things seemed unusually silent—like the place held its breath. Although Jake was certain it was only paranoia on his part, it seemed as if everyone he encountered turned the other way or tiptoed around him. He caught sight of Jude's secretary. Before she could get away, he handed her a stack of files without a word. If no one cared to talk to him, he wouldn't force himself upon them, but they would do their jobs.

"You have a visitor," she muttered as she stepped around him.

Jake shook his head and headed for the front lobby. His brother stood waiting with his hands clasped behind his back. His blond hair shimmered from the sunlight pouring through the huge windows behind him. Jake was slightly surprised to see Easton at Green's in the middle of the week. Since Easton's ex was the head of the law division, if Easton came to see Jake at work, he did so when Jake picked up a Saturday and there was no chance of running into Brad.

"Hey," Jake said, one arm hugging his brother.

"Hey, baby brother," Easton said, accepting his hug. "I came to see if you'd like to go to lunch."

In other words, he came to see if Jake would buy him lunch. Jake swept the room with his gaze, hoping against hope Brad didn't catch Easton there. Their breakup had been one hundred percent Easton's fault, but Easton was Jake's brother. He'd always take Easton's side. Still, he didn't want a confrontation. "Sure. Let's go."

Easton scanned the room. "Do you need to tell anyone you're leaving?"

Fuck. He hoped Easton wasn't here to start shit. Jake did not need that in his life right now. He'd purposely been avoiding his parents' calls and texts. If Easton got him fired, there would be no avoiding them. "Nope. We should hit that shrimp place on the beach."

"Oooh, I love that place," Easton said, fully vested. Jake knew how to distract Easton. He'd been keeping his brother happy his entire life, picking up the slack, and keeping Easton out of as much trouble as possible.

"Me too," Jake said, steering him toward the door. "I'll drive and you can tell me all about what you've been up to." Because Jake knew Easton. There was no such thing as a casual visit.

"Oh, good. I have so much to tell you."

Jake wasn't surprised. Easton was the great beauty of the family. His light coloration and flawless features had everyone's gaze skating over Jake and landing on Easton. If not for their eyes, no one would believe they were related. Easton was short and tiny. Blond and flirty. He smiled and people flocked to him. Jake was skinny and awkward. He didn't flirt nor did he have any clue how to start. At some unnamed point in Jake's life, he'd come to accept he would never stand outside Easton's shadow, even though he was a good eight inches taller than his older brother. If they weren't brothers, they probably wouldn't be friends either. Hell, he wasn't sure they were now. His dark thoughts managed to depress Jake on the way to the car. Somehow, he still managed to flash Easton the occasional smile as he rambled on about his recent visit to their family's country club. It wasn't until they made it halfway through lunch that Easton got to the heart of his visit.

"So, you know how Mom and Dad put that vacation home in the Hamptons in your name because you're the responsible brother?" Jake loved how Easton put air quotes around responsible. Somehow, Jake managed not to roll his eyes while Easton kept talking. "I realize they meant for us to share the place, but I never go there. So that's why I was thinking, maybe you could buy me out of my half?"

Jake's eye twitched. He rubbed it, praying the spasm didn't become a permanent one. Jake cleared his throat. Dealing with Easton was like brain surgery. It took a steady hand. "Well, they put the place in my name for political reasons. It's not actually ours to sell until they've passed on and selling it is the only way I could possibly give you half the value. I don't have Mom and Dad's kind of money."

"But you're a lawyer," Easton argued.

A genuine smile passed over Jake's lips. Sometimes it blew Jake away how little Easton knew about his life, or life in general, for that matter. "Not yet. I'm a paralegal. I haven't passed the bar exam, and even if I had, that wouldn't guarantee a huge salary."

"But when I lived with Brad, he had a huge salary."

Jake called on every ounce of patience he possessed. "Brad is the head of the legal department. I'm not."

"Oh." Easton looked crestfallen.

Fuck. This was how Easton did it. This was how he always got his way. "Is there a reason you were hoping I could give you half now?"

Easton brightened again. "I want to bake cakes."

Jake blinked. "Cakes." He heard his dry tone. There was no stopping it.

Easton nodded as if Jake's response had been a question and there'd been no trace of disbelief in Jake's voice. "Cheryl asked if I would make a cake for her little sister's birthday. At first, I was like, what the fuck do I know about baking? Surely she doesn't think I can make a fucking cake because I'm gay. Like, not every gay man is born the cake star or whatever. But then I was like, how hard can it be? So I did. And you know what?"

"What?" Jake said dutifully.

"It turned out amazing." Easton beamed with pride. "Cheryl went on and on about it. She even paid me two hundred dollars for it. That's when it hit me I could do this. It's easy. I'm good at it. But, as you know, it takes money to make money, so I'm trying to find a way to start my own bakery."

"Oh, sweetie. I'm sure you'll be amazing." Jake didn't have the heart to say anything else. He'd lost count of Easton's big ideas. All it took was the smallest praise to make Easton sure of his ability to take over the world. It was as endearing as it was sad. But Jake never lost hope that someday Easton would shock everyone and succeed. "Maybe you should start small. Bake from home and drum up a clientele."

Easton deflated again. "I can't do it from home. Marcus would see and he doesn't want me working. He says it's my job to be pretty and keep him happy. Having a working lover is classless. Obviously, that's not true, but he'd never let me work."

"Who in the hell is Marcus?"

"Oh, we just met."

Jake concentrated on breathing and keeping his

mind blank. No good could come of him showing his thoughts. Easton was in love with falling in love, except he wasn't the one falling. He was a bottomless well of neediness. All Jake could do was love his brother for the flighty mess he was and hope he never landed in the clutches of someone heartless.

"Where did you meet?"

A line formed between Easton's brows, as if he couldn't figure out why Jake asked. "At the country club, of course. He's a surgeon. You wouldn't like him."

Easton knew him well. Jake didn't usually like anyone Easton dated because he always chose men who chose Easton as a trophy. Then, once they met someone younger and hotter, Easton was out on his ass. The only exception had been Jake's boss, Brad. Brad had loved Easton blindly until the day he'd caught Easton cheating. Jake might've had a hand in that. He'd let Easton know Brad intended to propose. Easton had done the rest. No one would ever tie Easton down. Brad hated Jake for his brother's sins. The man would never see the situation for what it was—Jake had saved him. Now Brad had a nice guy. Someone who matched Brad's heart. Easton would never be that person.

"It's probably not a great idea to start a relationship by hiding a business."

Easton shrugged while picking at his plate. "It's not like it'll matter in six months."

No, it wouldn't. Marcus wouldn't last that long. Jake listened to Easton's happy chatter through the rest of their meal. By the time they said their goodbyes in the parking lot of Green's, Jake's mood was complete shit. He loved his brother so much. Jake wished he would grow up. Easton was the older brother. He should be the responsible one. Jake also wished Easton would meet someone nice and really fall in love or become the most successful baker on the west coast. Anything at all was better than flirting his way through life like it was pointless. Jake was powerless to do anything but hope.

"Mr. Hollister would like to see you in his office." Sheila's words penetrated his thoughts and pulled Jake's mind away from his usual worry over Easton. He never got called to Brad's office. Jake couldn't even think of any reason why he would be now.

"Thanks, Sheila." He headed down the hall. At Brad's office, he knocked on the open door.

Brad glanced up. His expression gave nothing away. "Come in and shut the door behind you, please." Damn. That didn't sound good. Jake did as bade. Brad motioned at the empty chair across from his desk. "Have a seat." Fuck. Brad's tone made Jake nervous as hell. Thankfully, Brad didn't make him suffer long. He dove in the moment Jake's ass hit the seat. "I got a call this morning from your mother." Surely there was nothing more horrifying, but Jake didn't say as much. "She wanted to know why I hadn't accepted your resignation from the team." Jake stood corrected. It was more horrific than he first thought. Brad kept talking, finding new depths of humiliation for Jake. "I didn't say anything right away because I wasn't sure how to react. Since I never received a formal resignation letter from you, I was obviously surprised to learn you were quitting. After giving it some thought, I realized maybe it's for the best." Jake's heartbeat pounded in his ears. This was a nightmare. He'd hoped—if he ignored his parents—this would go away. Jake had never expected his mother would go this far to have her way. Now Brad was saying it was for the best. Jake couldn't find his voice. Brad didn't seem to need him for this conversation. "When you first started working here, everything meshed really well. After things ended with Easton, you haven't seemed to be as thrilled to be here. I know that family is important. You have to do right by yours. But we also need team players working to ensure Green's is a success. All of our jobs depend on it. I don't think you can work efficiently with me and still feel loyal to your brother." Brad took a breath. Jake felt the hammer before it fell. "Please have your desk cleaned out by the end of the day."

A lifetime of training saved Jake. He'd never been allowed to show real emotion. That rigid life came to his rescue now. He could be a professional. "This has been an amazing opportunity." He stood. "It won't take me until the end of the day to clear out."

Before Jake could make his getaway, Brad spoke up, stopping him. He sounded uncomfortable as hell. "Normally, Human Resources would've taken care of this, but—in this case—I chose to handle it. I don't want you to leave here thinking it's because I wanted to be the one who saw you out. That's not true. At one time, we were friends. We were almost family." Brad took a breath. Jake couldn't blink. Brad looked almost sad. That didn't make sense. "I know your parents. They were almost my in-laws. I understand they have expectations. The thing is, I've always secretly hoped you'd do something else. Find your path."

A snort escaped Jake before he knew it would

happen. It was too late. The flood gates were opening. "You think I should just say no to them and skip away."

Brad's expression never changed. He was obviously uncomfortable, but he didn't back down. "Yes. Open your mouth and say no. If not, I worry what will happen to you one day when you realize your life is gone and you wasted it on someone else's dream. I hope you see this as a new door opening. Maybe don't tell them right away and I won't take another call from your family. If nothing else, take some time to think before making your next move. You can't have back the years wasted."

Like the seven years Brad wasted on Easton. Jake could've said anything during those years. Saved Brad sooner. Maybe the real truth was, Jake hadn't wanted things to be exactly as they were now. Brad hated him and he'd been one of the few people in the world who understood Jake. It was funny how far people would go to cling to anything real when surrounded by fakes. This would be the last time they spoke. Jake should explain, but he'd never learned to be real. He'd never been allowed to be himself. Maybe there wasn't a genuine version of him. Perhaps he was every bit as phony as everyone else in his family.

His chin dipped, acknowledging Brad's words, and his mouth opened. Even Jake didn't know what he'd say.

"I was the one who got their heart broken when you broke up with my family." Jake blinked. Whoa. He'd not expected to admit that. It was like he could hear himself speaking, but he couldn't control the words. A dam had cracked inside him. He couldn't stop the bitterness seeping out. "I was really the one you dumped. I was in high school when you started dating Easton. You were the only nice person in my life. The only person who ever looked directly at me while speaking and talked to me instead of at me. When you got me the job here, I thought we were truly friends. It wasn't until you looked at me with the same hatred you have for Easton that I realized you don't see me any clearer than anyone else does. Otherwise, you would've realized I fucking saved you and you wouldn't have left me alone in this goddamn family." The hatred between them went both ways, it seemed. Jake took a breath. He didn't feel better. It was possible that was why he never bothered speaking his mind. Words never changed a damn thing for him. "Thank you for the opportunity to be a part of this team. I'll think about what you said." He turned away.

"Jake."

Jake didn't slow, even though Brad's quietly spoken tone cut him to the bone. He didn't have very much here. He shouldn't even need a box. Still, he needed every drop of his remaining strength for the upcoming walk of shame to the parking lot. Jake had nothing left to give Brad today. Sometimes he wondered if he had anything to give anyone. It was possible he wasn't fake like his parents. Instead, he was just empty. Hollow. At twenty-six, Jake had already given every ounce of himself in the fight to stay alive beneath the weight of a crushing existence. Now he was too tired to cope.

THE VIBRATION IN FLYNN'S BACK POCKET pulled him from the rhythm he'd found while hammering. He pulled his phone out while wiping the sweat from his brow. The number flashing on the screen didn't look familiar, but next to no one had this number. No one called unless they knew him. With a shrug, he hit the answer button and switched to speaker phone. He used the hem of his shirt to wipe his face as he answered.

"Alright?"

There was a moment of dead air. "Is that really how you answer the phone?"

A snort escaped Flynn. Even though Brad had never called him before, Flynn recognized the man's sophisticated tone. "The Scot in me runs deep. Are you really expecting a hello, how may I direct your call today?" Flynn faked an exaggerated nasally American accent. He smiled at the sound of Brad's sexy chuckle.

"I had to fire Jake today."

Flynn's smile fell. Brad had gone from laughter to a pained-sounding confession in a heartbeat. "Oh."

"I thought, since he's yours and Jake doesn't know how to reach out for help, I'd better call."

"Aye. Thank you. He will nae take it well, even though it's for the best." Flynn cleared his throat as he realized how much his accent thickened.

"No. I think it's safe to say he didn't take it well."

Flynn hated that anything bad happened to Jake. It didn't matter Jake was miserable at that job or that he needed to let the place go; no one like getting fired. Flynn imagined it would be even worse for a perfectionist like Jake. "Thanks for letting me know. I'll take care of him."

"I know you will." Brad's words were oddly

flattering. Flynn had never done anything to give Brad a good opinion of him. He'd openly flirted with Brad's man, Kato, more times than he could count. He'd always believed jealousy was a great motivator and Kato needed someone to love him as is. Flynn was an excellent judge of character. Brad and Kato were meant to be. Just as Jake had been destined to meet Flynn. This would definitely be one of those times he'd have to prove why. Jake wouldn't easily open up about how much losing a job he fucking hated hurt. Steps made in the right direction were often the most terrifying.

THREE

ONCE AGAIN, Jake found himself sitting in the parking lot at the Den of Payne with no memory of the drive. He'd told Flynn he wouldn't come here again. If he'd been in his right mind, he wouldn't have. Jake was hard pressed to articulate exactly why getting fired gutted him. He stared at the nondescript building and search for an explanation. Some string of words that would spell out the reason he felt like everything was gone. Without warning, his eyes stung, forcing him to blink away tears. His parents would have their way now. They'd leave him penniless, and if he didn't fall in line, homelessness would come next. No doubt, in a few short weeks, he'd be neck deep in the trenches at Smith, Smith, and Tate. Craig Smith would report his every move to Jake's parents. His time with Flynn was over.

"We keep meeting this way."

The muffled yell had Jake nearly jumping from his skin. His gaze shot to the window. Payne stood on the other. Jake hit the button, removing the barrier between them.

Like last time, heat filled Jake's cheeks. His face was on fire. "Sorry."

Payne didn't look as hard today. He wore the expression of a loving parent. Jake's throat burned. No one looked at him that way. That was exactly why he knew the expression. He'd dreamed of seeing it just once on his father's face. "Flynn doesn't work here anymore. He quit about three months ago. It was the same day you were here last, come to think of it." Jake's brain froze, but Payne's lips kept moving, oblivious to their destructive powers. "If you'd like, I could give you a two-day pass and you could meet some of the other masters. You might find someone you like."

Jake scrambled for something to save him. Anything at all. His gaze shot in every direction before landing on a nearby park bench. Kato sat alone, fidgeting with a bag on his lap.

"No. Thank you, though. I'm not here for

Flynn," he lied. Jake motioned Kato's way. "I'm here for him."

Payne's expression cleared. "Oh. That's good. That makes me feel less guilty about not being able to leave right now." Jake didn't know what that meant. He was just glad his lie sounded plausible. "Maybe another day we'll lure you into our services."

Jake flashed Payne a fake smile at the offer. "Maybe so. I'll talk it over with Flynn." Every word leaving his lips was bullshit. Flynn had quit. He'd quit three months ago. Yet he kept leaving Jake's bed each morning to go to work. Jake had blindly believed him each time. After all, he had no reason to question Flynn's honesty.

Payne waved as he walked away. Jake kept his gaze locked on Kato. He sat alone on the bench. Jake swiped his palms on his jeans. An inner battle raged. This was Brad's soon-to-be husband. Nothing good could come of Jake approaching him. Kato's terrified expression had Jake forgetting the man probably hated him on principle. He threw open his car door and headed Kato's way.

"Do you need help?"

A smile touched Kato's lips. It didn't reach his eyes. "I'm good. Thank you."

Jake moved closer and claimed the empty spot on

the bench beside Kato. "Are you waiting for someone? It's Jake, by the way," he added, hoping to ease Kato's open discomfort. "We met at your engagement party."

Kato didn't look his way. Since he was blind, Jake wasn't insulted. "I'm waiting on a ride. You're dating Flynn, right?"

For a moment, Jake waffled between admitting he wouldn't call them dating and reminding Kato he was Easton's brother. Both options left him with a bad taste in his mouth. In the end, he chose to dodge. "I came looking for Flynn. It seems he quit, which you'd think I'd know." Even Jake heard the defeat in his voice. "But I guess not," he added lamely.

"That's..." Kato visibly fought for something to say, making Jake feel like twice the ass.

Jake rushed to change the subject. "I could give you a ride, if you're tired of waiting."

Kato's obvious discomfort seemed to double. "Um..."

"Never mind," Jake said, coming to his feet. He didn't know how to be normal. Kato probably half expected no one would ever find his body if he went with Jake. "I don't know what I was thinking. No one in their right mind would accept a ride from the brother of their fiancé's ex who also just got fired by that same fiancé. Sorry to have bothered you." Jake took two steps toward his car.

"Brad fired you?"

Jake paused. He shrugged before he realized what he'd done. Jake shook his head at his idiocy and used his words instead. "Yeah. To be fair, he wasn't wrong. Things haven't been the same since..." Jake didn't want to go down that path. No one liked discussing exes.

"I don't envy your position," Kato said, sounding surprisingly pragmatic. "It's not easy to be trapped between needing to earn a living and keeping everyone appeased."

"Especially someone like Easton," Jake said before he realized it would happen. Guilt slammed into him. He sounded disloyal. "I guess I should go."

"Actually," Kato said, stopping him from running away. "I'm sort of low on my mom's list of priorities today and Brad has a late meeting. Plus, Detroit is out of town for a fight and Payne has clients today, so he can't leave. I could use a ride home." Kato bit his lip as if it had taken everything he had to ask for help. He looked sweet. It was no wonder Brad had fallen like a ton of bricks for Kato. He seemed to be everything Easton wasn't. Everything Brad deserved.

"Sure." Jake hesitated as Kato came to his feet.

He was out of his depth. "Do you need to hold on to me or anything? I'm sorry if I come off as dumb. In truth, I'm socially inept to a painful extreme." Even to Jake's ears, he sounded like a complete moron and uncomfortable as hell.

Kato's blinding smile washed away the awkwardness. "If you don't mind, I could use your help."

Jake awkwardly took Kato's arm and led him toward his car. "So," Jake said, scrambling to make the situation less uncomfortable. "How much longer until your wedding?"

"Two weeks." He sounded excited. Jake thought that was nice. He'd never get to marry anyone most likely. Not anyone he wanted anyhow.

"I'm glad Brad met you," Jake said for lack of anything else as he helped Kato into the passenger's seat. He closed the door before Kato responded. Jake berated himself as he circled the car. As Easton's brother, he needed to pretend Kato wasn't connected to Brad. Kato was just someone Jake helped out because he needed a ride. Brad wasn't his friend anymore and Easton would always be his brother. By the time he slid behind the wheel, Jake had shut himself back inside his usual box.

Kato wasn't having it. "You're very different from

your brother. Not that I have anything against Easton," Kato quickly added. "I'm not the type to hold grudges and it's not like I can pretend Brad was single before he started dating me. What I mean is, you're opposites in a lot of ways."

Jake nodded. He pulled away from the curb before it occurred to him that Kato couldn't see his head bob. This was his first time holding a conversation with a blind man. He kept forgetting his voice. "Yes. We're very different. Easton is a free spirit. I'm not."

A deep chuckle rumbled from Kato's side of the car. "Yet you're the one dating Flynn, while I have a feeling Easton would be traumatized if someone spanked him."

A smile snapped to Jake's lips. For all Easton's rebellion, he was as vanilla as they came. "Thank you for that." He was sure Kato didn't understand why his words made Jake happy. Until Kato made the observation, Jake hadn't realized there was something about him that didn't follow the rules. At his core, he wasn't the perfect son and brother. While Jake was alone with Flynn, Jake was fearless and unique. Easton was—no doubt—normal and uptight all the time despite his unwillingness to fall into line with their parents' rules.

"I doubt Easton would've offered to help me either."

Kato's claim didn't steal Jake's newfound humor. "Oh, he would take you home if you needed him, but he'd cut you to the bone with sly insults the whole way. Easton is..." Jake tried to think of a way to describe his brother without being insulting or disloyal. After all, Jake loved Easton. In a lot of ways, it was them against the world. But Jake wasn't blind to his brother's faults. Easton wasn't perfect.

"He's your brother," Kato said, rescuing him. "You don't get to choose your family, but they're yours. I have a brother who's only eighteen and is already the biggest man whore you'll ever meet. Like seriously, it's bad. He's quarterback for a college team, so he's hopping from every bed. It's embarrassing, and I'd fight anyone else who dared to say that about him." Kato's hands lifted before falling back to his lap. "He's mine. Easton is yours. You don't have to explain."

Jake discovered something about himself—he liked Kato. He was truly grateful Brad had found a nice guy. Jake would drop Kato at home and turn the page on this chapter of his life. He still felt like a complete loser with no idea where he was headed, but he wouldn't look back on anything with bitterness. Except for maybe the fact that Flynn had quit his job and lied for the past three months. Yeah, there was still that.

After five minutes of ringing the doorbell and knocking, Flynn accepted Jake wasn't home. That didn't stop him turning over a nearby pot for the spare key. After letting himself in, he re-hid the key and disarmed the alarm. He should probably wait outside or let Jake know he was there. Flynn didn't have any intentions of giving Jake a chance to turn him away. He knew Jake. After a day like today, Jake would try shoving him away to deal with things on his own. He'd swallow his feelings no matter how much he choked. Flynn wasn't having it. He knew Jake didn't see getting let go as the blessing it was, but Flynn saw. If Flynn backed away now, Jake would be at another law firm by this time next week, pretending he wasn't unhappy. No way did Flynn intend to let that happen.

Flynn wasted no time stripping down to only his jeans. He sat on the couch and waited. Jake came through the door staring at his feet. His gaze didn't move Flynn's way as he peeled off his jacket and tossed it across the chair by the door. When he finally spoke, his voice sounded hollow.

"I didn't know you were coming."

Even Flynn could feel the intensity of his stare as he willed Jake to look at him. Still, Jake refused. "You didn't call when you were let go or you would've known. Instead, I had to hear it from Brad."

If Jake was the least bit surprised, he didn't show it. Instead, Jake toed off his shoes and loosened his tie. "Are we telling each other things now? I wasn't sure, since you didn't tell me you'd quit the Den of Payne."

Flynn couldn't let Jake pick a fight. All that would accomplish was making Jake feel worse. Flynn needed Jake's happiness. Sometimes daddies had to demand that. "Take off your clothes but leave on your underwear."

At his harsh tone, Jake's gaze finally swung his way. His sexy green eyes gave nothing away. He looked the same as he had the first time Flynn had ever demanded this of him—like he wouldn't be budged. "I'll pass."

His face hardened. Flynn felt it happen. His tone deepened to match his darkening mood. "That wasn't a request. You told me you would never go back to the Den of Payne. Yet you just admitted you broke your word. I told you there was nothing there for you. You are mine. You don't visit places like that. Strip to your underwear and come here. Now, Jacob Wayne Woods." He saw Jake's throat move as he swallowed. Flynn knew he'd won. His hands moved to the buttons on his shirt. Flynn settled in. His gaze soaked up the sight of Jake slowly stripping down to his hot pink bikini briefs that only held back his erection due to placement. Flynn's cock stirred. Water filled his mouth. All it would take was the tiniest tug and Jake's erection would spring free of the material barely containing him. Flynn patted his lap. Jake followed his silent command. The moment his ass hit Flynn's lap, Flynn urged him sideways.

He wrapped his arms around Jake, leaving Jake no other choice than to accept his comfort. "I'm so sorry, baby. You should've called me the second you left that place."

"I couldn't think straight," Jake admitted in a small voice. "One second, I was leaving. The next, I was sitting in the Den of Payne's parking lot. I didn't call, but my body knew to take me to you."

Flynn kissed his temple. "I've got you now, baby boy. Everything will be okay." His hand slid down Jake's body. Flynn stroked Jake's cock through his underwear, shaping his erection before moving lower. He massaged Jake's balls. It was the lightest of touches. The perfect amount of pressure to purposefully drive Jake insane. Jake's lips parted on a pant. Flynn's gaze locked on the sight. He focused on every hard breath and facial tic, following Jake's lead. His legs moved restlessly. Flynn applied a hint more pressure but still moved slow. He rubbed Jake's hard dick, staying outside his underwear. The material was soaked with pre-cum. It got wetter by the second. Flynn's cock twitched like it was the one being tortured. Jake's entire body jerked as Flynn dragged his short fingernails up Jake's length. His hips lifted. Flynn held him still.

"You don't need more, baby boy. Spread your knees." Jake whimpered but did as told. Flynn fingered his crack, pressing against Jake's asshole, teasing him. "You're so beautiful right now," Flynn praised. "I know you want to beg, but you know it's useless." Jake's balls were drawn up tight. Flynn stroked them. "There's more pleasure in waiting than most people realize. Everyone is so focused on the orgasm. They don't think about the experience." He lightly trailed his fingertips up and down Jake's cock. "They don't close their eyes and feel. This isn't sex. I'm not jacking you off. My intent isn't to feel your cum dripping from me as quickly as possible." Jake moaned. Flynn didn't let up. "I want to touch a piece of you no one else has. My only goal is everything. I want you to feel everything and know that I own you. You could push my hand away and tug yourself into orgasm to spite me, but I know you want this." He dipped his finger beneath the waistband of Jake's underwear and stroked Jake's crown. The sound Jake made, and his expression, nearly caused Flynn to blow without touching his dick. He swore he could feel everything Jake felt. "Focus on the sensations, baby boy. Close your eyes and feel. Then tell me everything you'd do without hesitation in this moment."

Jake took an audible breath. He moved against Flynn's palm. With his eyes closed, he looked completely focused. Jake licked his lips. "I want to straddle your hips and let your dick stretch me wide." Flynn swore he couldn't blink while watching Jake's lips move, giving him the images inside his head. "There's a toy in my drawer. It's battery-operated and feels exactly like it's sucking my dick. I'd keep that on me while you fuck me hard. One orgasm isn't enough. I try to pretend the first one didn't happen, even though I know you feel it. But I don't want to stop. You feel too good. Mean too much." Flynn stopped breathing at Jake's confession.

He clung to every word. "I want your soul too." Jake whimpered. His agitation grew. "I need the connection of our bodies, skin on skin. It's the only time I think you feel anything for me. I need that. You're the only one who has what I need. The second orgasm builds. I bury my face against your neck because I need your scent as much as I need to hide in your protective embrace. My lips brush your neck with every whispered word I chant."

Flynn's cock jumped and dripped like he was receiving the world's greatest head. His eyes burned from barely blinking as he stared at Jake's face. "What are you whispering?"

Jake's entire body stiffened. His features hardened. A loud gasp rang through the air as his body jerked. One word joined the air leaving Jake's lungs. "Daddy."

SOMETHING SNAPPED INSIDE JAKE AS HE FILLED his underwear with cum. The submissive inside him disappeared, leaving behind someone who wanted Flynn's cock in his ass and didn't care to wait. Jake rolled to his knees and peeled off his soaked underwear. He tugged at the button on Flynn's jeans. His gaze never wavered from his task. He was beyond asking for permission. Jake had been good too long. Taken orders too many times. He needed Flynn's dick, and he planned to get it. Air filled his lungs as Flynn's cock filled his hand. Without a thought, he dropped his head and sucked Flynn's dick like his life depended upon it. When Flynn's erection was soaked with saliva, Jake straddled Flynn's hips and captured his mouth. He was more than half out of his head. Rational thought was a thing of the past. When he tried teasing Flynn into fucking him, Flynn gently pushed him away.

"Wait. I need a condom. We have to keep you safe, baby boy."

In his haze of insanity, Flynn's words didn't make sense. He nearly cried out his frustration. They needed to be one. Jake couldn't stand another minute of this. Flynn locked his arms around Jake's waist and stood. Jake locked his legs around Flynn and let the man carry him to bed. When his back hit the mattress, some of the madness subsided. Flynn didn't tease or make him wait. He lubed Jake's asshole, suited up, and slipped inside. Jake's eyes unexpectedly filled with tears. His teeth chattered. The shock of the day hit him full force. To his horror, a tear slid from the corner of his eye. Jake clenched his teeth, hoping to hold back the emotions overwhelming him. He thought life had killed his ability to feel a long time ago. Jake was so focused on trying to shore up his wall, he didn't notice right away that Flynn was squeezing him to his chest. Light kisses swept across his temple before moving to his ear.

Flynn's lips brushed the shell of his ear. "Shhh, baby boy. I've got you."

Jake swallowed hard. The panic didn't subside. His tongue betrayed him. "Do you?" He felt Flynn go still. Jake couldn't stop. "You're not mine. I shouldn't care, but you're not. Someday, you'll be gone and then what? I don't even have a job now. There's no choice but to do what my parents want." Each word came out faster than the next. Flynn couldn't control it. "Soon I'll be trapped in a world I hate without even these moments to save me. I should accept it, but I don't know how. One day, you'll stop showing up and I have no right to complain. I'm just another body to you. It's not fair to you that I care, but I do. I want to matter to one fucking person. You can't even be honest with me about where you go. Every day, you say you're going to work, but you quit the Den of Payne and didn't tell me. It's like I don't even matter enough to tell me that. I'm just nothing."

Flynn's mouth found Jake's, cutting off the tirade.

The fight bled from Jake. He was exhausted. His shoulders hurt from being tensed for years. Flynn's tongue stroked his. The kiss was slow and methodical. Jake let it happen. He was too weak to deny himself this one good thing, even though it was temporary.

"Let's clean you up, baby," Flynn said with his lips brushing lightly across Jake's. "I need to show you something."

Fear had Jake scrambling. Flynn couldn't walk away unsatisfied. Jake had nothing else to offer. If he couldn't keep Flynn pleased, someone else would. He held on to Flynn, refusing to let him pull away. "I don't want you to stop."

"Shhh," Flynn soothed against the corner of Jake's mouth. He swiped Jake's hair away from Jake's face, stroking him and calming him. "You need me to stop," Flynn said, ripping out Jake's heart. He was failing at everything.

"Please?" Even Jake heard the desperation in his voice. "I don't have anything else to offer. There's nothing else about me you could possibly want." As he gave his darkest thoughts a voice, Jake's arms slipped away. It was like his body gave up before his mouth. He wouldn't beg anymore. His chest hurt too much. Flynn's gaze bored into Jake's skin. Jake didn't even have the strength to meet Flynn's stare.

"Is that really how you feel? Do you honestly believe I only come around for sex?"

In truth, it sounded a bit dumb when Flynn said it aloud. Flynn could have anyone. Jake strongly suspected he'd already had everyone. Why would he waste his time with Jake?

"No. I don't know why you come around."

Flynn moved away and shifted positions until he sat next to Jake, facing him. It was the first time Jake had ever seen Flynn look hurt. He hadn't thought he could feel worse, but with one look at Flynn's wounded expression, Jake found depression's basement subfloor.

"I come around because I want to spend time with you. What the fuck? I thought you knew that." Flynn looked away. His gaze stayed glued to a spot across the room, as if he could no longer look at Jake. Jake's throat swelled to nearly closing. Flynn was the one person he couldn't stomach hurting.

He touched Flynn's knee. "Flynn." He needed

Flynn to look at him and make everything better. His distance was killing Jake.

Flynn refused to look his way. "Get cleaned up." Flynn's hard tone left no doubt his words were an order.

Jake pressed his hand to his stomach, wishing the butterflies would stop. He couldn't lose Flynn—liar or not. That was how sad Jake had become—how desperate for any affection at all. He'd take a liar over loneliness any day. With his head down, Jake headed for the bathroom. He wondered if the pains in his chest were a heart attack. Maybe he should be calling for the paramedics. Jake went through the motions of showering on auto-pilot. His mind refused to work right. Everything was a haze until he stepped out of the bathroom and found Flynn lacing up his work boots. "You're leaving." It wasn't a question. The dead note to Jake's tone was one he felt all the way to his soul. He'd known they weren't forever. Still, he hadn't prepared himself for their inevitable end.

Flynn glanced up at Jake's appearance. His gaze skirted down Jake's nude body. There wasn't an ounce of interest in his eyes. Flynn was in full punishment mode. Jake knew the cold shoulder when he saw it. Or maybe Flynn was just done. He'd had his fun and now Jake had turned into more work than he was worth. Damn. They really were over. Jake wished he kept clothes in his bathroom so he wouldn't have to do this completely exposed in every way.

"You're coming too. Get dressed."

Jake blinked at Flynn's order. "Where am I going?"

"Get dressed," Flynn repeated, sounding tired.

Without another word, Jake moved to the dresser and found some clothes. He didn't pick and choose. Jake grabbed the first thing he found. Since it seemed like he always rotated the top four outfits in the drawers, it was a t-shirt and jeans he wore all the time. He dressed in silence while doing his damnedest not to look Flynn's way. With his head down, Jake followed Flynn to his truck. He stopped when Flynn stopped and moved when Flynn urged him to move. Jake didn't care where they were going. Until Flynn forgave him, nothing mattered any longer. He couldn't even find the strength to lift his gaze from his lap as Flynn drove. It was as if all his strength had been zapped away.

When Flynn put the truck in park, Jake found his eyes lifting without thought. They sat in the empty parking lot of a white stone business with no sign. It was dark inside. Flynn jumped out and circled the truck, freeing Jake. He followed Flynn to the door. His curiosity rose by the second and doubled when Jake unlocked the front door. As they stepped inside, Jake was overcome by the scent of wood and sawdust—like someone had been building something inside. Flynn flipped a switch, illuminating the room. The place was empty except for a long bar, stacks of wood, and tools. It looked as if someone had been using the space to build shelves.

Jake turned in a circle, eyeing everything. It looked like the building had once been used as a bar or club of some type but was now stripped bare. "What is this place?"

Flynn flashed him a smile. "I know you like to read, but do you also like hearing sordid tales?"

Jake couldn't resist the teasing note to Flynn's voice. Relief poured through him. It didn't seem like Flynn was still angry with him. Jake jumped at the chance to keep him happy. "Of course."

Flynn's smile brightened. He winked. "Good. This place has one. You see, several years back, there was this seventeen-year-old who always got into something. Usually, it was out of boredom, but on this night, it was to impress his friends. Anyhow, there was a popular hotel in the highlands. It was a huge place always filled with tourists. Even though it was a small village, the loch drew travelers year-round. Plus, the place had a pub inside that was always busy with locals as well. The drinking age in Scotland is eighteen inside an establishment unless accompanied by an adult, then it's sixteen. Not that any of that matters; this lad was poor. He couldn't afford to drink." Flynn leaned against the counter and stared at a spot in the distance, as if only seeing what was inside his head. "Late one Saturday night, when the crowd had died down and the servers were busy straightening the place for the night, he sneaked behind the bar and nicked a bottle of whiskey. Unfortunately, before he made it outside, a burly fellow nabbed him and carried him in to see the owner." Jake was fascinated by Flynn's expression. He looked years younger. "The fellow who owned the place, William Thomson, was just in his early forties. He was a huge man with bulging muscles and a barrel chest. Even though he was a good six inches shorter than the teen, he was like an ox. William took one look at the boy, dismissed his thugs, and turned the lad over his knee." Flynn barked out a laugh. His eyes shone bright with mirth. He swiped at them. "That's when things took a turn. He's whaling on the boy's arse and it hits him—the lad's erection is poking him in the leg, and it's moans he's hearing instead of wails. That's the night the lad became his baby boy and William became a daddy." Flynn's expression closed. His gaze stayed locked on a place only he could see. "The townsfolk didn't like that one bit. People still flooded the pub, but they watched him out the corner of their eyes, thinking they should be hiding their boys. By the time the boy was nineteen, the pair had long passed had enough of the intolerance. William sold the hotel for a huge sum. Of course, being as how he was already Plockton's only millionaire, he didn't need the money. Still, they took their newly padded bank account and moved to the States." Flynn straightened away from the bar. He drew a circle in the air with his finger. "They opened this place together, working side by side for the next twenty years until William passed peacefully in his sleep from an undiagnosed heart ailment."

Flynn's smile turned sad. His gaze slid Jake's way and lingered. "With William gone, I had no reason to keep the place open. All I had was his money and the knowledge of being a master that he'd passed on to me. I went to work for the Den of Payne, but I hung on to this place." Flynn's gaze skirted away again. Jake's throat swelled at the loss in Flynn's eyes. "For a long time, I questioned why I couldn't part with a building that brought me nothing but extra bills. But this was ours and I couldn't sell it. I couldn't drive past this place and see new people inside, knowing William would never walk through the door again. There's a part of me that's always believed William would give me a sign. That, from beyond the grave, he'd still find a way to tell me what to do." Flynn focused on him, and Jake couldn't look away. "Then, you came to me crushed beneath the weight of expectations. You said all you wanted was to see my face." Flynn's mouth lifted in one corner. "William used to say that to me every day. He always said he didn't need anything else. I knew then what I was meant to do. So, welcome to your bookstore. Once I'm finished remodeling it, of course. What would you like to name the place?"

Jake blinked. Flynn still stared at him expectantly. He blinked again. Nothing changed. "Um."

"That's unique, but I'm not sure anyone will know what the place is with that name."

"I don't understand." Jake hated sounding like an idiot, but nothing made sense any longer.

"Baby Boy's Books, it is."

Flynn's refusal to be real had Jake's voice rushing

back. "You can't give me a store. I don't know anything about owning a store."

"I can. I just did, and—as it happens—I know a great deal about running a business. You've got nothing to worry about. I intend to be with you every step of the way."

"You don't understand. I just got fired. It'll be a while before this place is ready and making money. I have a small savings, but nothing for anything like this." He could get money from his parents, but not for something like this. Hell would freeze before they gave him a dime that didn't go toward something they preapproved.

Flynn's smile turned into a laugh. "I don't know how many different ways you need me to tell you that I've got you. William left me everything. I've no reason to ever work a day other than pure boredom. This is all for you. I will take care of you."

For a full minute Jake floundered before finding his voice again. "But...why?"

Flynn shook his head. His expression screamed that Jake was a moron. He closed the distance between them and took Jake's hands. He walked backward while holding Jake's stare. "Because I love you, you daft idiot. Even though I've never met anyone blinder, you're still the most amazing man

I've met in a long while. I don't think you understand how rare and beautiful you are." Jake hung on every word, scared to believe. "Our relationship is unique. I know you don't see it, but I also know you never found this before me. Like I only found it once before you. Let me do this for you. Come live with me and let everything else go. You don't have to live a life that doesn't fit. Run away from everything with me. Do this."

The hopeful glint in Flynn's eyes had Jake's good sense flying out the window. Flynn loved him. Wow. That was so much more than Jake ever expected.

"Did you really quit your job to do this for me?"

Flynn nodded. "I can afford to be impulsive."

Whoa. That was insane and... damn. Jake was blown away. He looked away. His mind whirled. He could see this place filled with books, smelling like heaven. This was so fast. Everything was changing too quickly. Fuck, he really wanted to throw caution and good sense to the wind. How much of this was pity? They'd only been together six months. Surely Flynn didn't want him living with him. He could pay his bills a few months comfortably without help. There was a real chance he could do this.

Jake's gaze slid back to Flynn's hopeful face. "Okay." He held up his hand before Flynn's smile could become an explosion. "But I'm not moving in with you. That's too much. Otherwise, as long as you let me genuinely pull my weight in this partnership, I'm in."

Some of the happiness dimmed in Flynn's expression, confusing Jake. "I'm so proud of you."

The backs of Jake's eyes stung. Before Flynn, he'd never heard those words. Flynn never let him down. His fingers found the hem of Flynn's t-shit. He twisted the material, balling it in his hand, before slowly towing Flynn closer. He held Flynn's stare. "I'm sorry about my breakdown earlier."

"You were due," Flynn said, dismissing his apology.

Jake shook his head. "Don't do that. I said things that hurt you. You deserve better from me. I left you hanging. Knowing that is sort of choking me now. I need your happiness."

"I'm happy."

Even though Jake knew Flynn was serious, he was too. They'd left the bed angry and hurt. He couldn't have that. His gaze moved to Flynn's lips. They were still swollen from their heated session. Need filled Jake. Flynn had confessed to loving him. Jake had to take a breath. He was so fucking moved by Flynn and every wonderful thing he did. There was no reason for Flynn to love him. Jake hadn't earned that. "I think you should make love to me."

Flynn's sexy full lips quirked in the corner. "I will. Just not here in the sawdust and dirt. My baby doesn't get treated like that."

Jake's hands slid across Flynn's hips. He drew Flynn even closer, ensuring the man felt exactly how hot Jake was for him. "The parking lot is dark and empty. Your Suburban has a really roomy back. I'm betting the seats even fold down."

"You can wait until we get home, brat."

Jake pretended to pout all the way home. He broke the moment he found himself nude and across Flynn's lap in bed. The sting of Flynn's palm against Jake's ass had moans vibrating from Jake's throat and his cock leaking on Flynn's thighs. Flynn fell backward across Jake's mattress. He urged Jake to straddle his hips as he pulled Jake's mouth down to his. Their tongues stroked. The needy sounds Flynn made vibrated around Jake's tongue. His heart was full. Jake hadn't felt like anyone was in his corner in a long time. Knowing Flynn loved him and planned to have his back added a new layer to making love. Jake felt like Flynn belonged to him. Calling Flynn daddy wasn't just a game. He was cared for in a way he hadn't been before Flynn came around.

Their sweat-covered bodies clung in all the right places. Flynn squeezed Jake's ass as he rocked Jake against him. Their erections moved together in the most delicious ways.

"Jake." Flynn's whisper punched Jake in the chest. Not only did Flynn rarely call him by his name, the desperation of the single word called on Jake's deep-seeded desire to keep Flynn happy. "I need you."

Jake's stomach muscles cramped. Those three words were even more powerful than words of love. "Tell me, sexy. What do you need?"

Flynn bit Jake's bottom lip before doing as Jake asked. "I need to feel you inside me."

Everything inside Jake screeched to a halt, including his heart. They'd never really discussed this before. Jake always went with the flow. Being a top was a bit out of his comfort zone. Flynn tended to always keep him on the other side of comfort. But Jake feared there was nowhere he wouldn't go for Flynn. To hide his fear of failing, Jake concentrated on licking Flynn's nipple. He took a breath. Flynn's hands lightly ran up Jake's back. Jake's eyes fell closed. He loved this man with everything. His jaw hardened with determination. Jake forced his thoughts into silence and sat back on his heels. Flynn was showing him a huge amount of trust. Jake wouldn't let him regret it. He suited up and coated the condom with lube. With no voice inside his head to betray him, Jake's body burned. Flynn looked turned on and ready to beg. Jake's hunger grew by the second. So too did his pride. He was the one who made Flynn hot. No one else got to see Flynn like this. He owned Flynn right now. In a second, he would claim the man's body as his.

Jake palmed Flynn's leaking cock. "You're beautiful." He stroked. Flynn gasped for air. Jake shifted positions and urged Flynn's thighs apart. He held Flynn's stare through every second. Jake needed Flynn to see there was nothing he wouldn't do to please him.

He pushed his way inside. Jake almost came immediately. Between the sound Flynn made and the way Flynn's ass squeezed him, Jake nearly lost it. Flynn had changed him. Jake saw it a little more every day. Each time he looked in the mirror, he recognized himself a little less. He'd gone from wondering if he was capable of feeling anything to feeling everything. Jake didn't want it to stop. Flynn had him addicted to experiencing life.

The world tilted. In a flash, Jake found himself on his back with Flynn straddling him. He rode Jake's dick, taking what he wanted. His teeth sank and tugged at Jake's skin. He bit and sucked, while Jake fought for sanity. There was pleasure in the pain. Jake knew there would be marks covering his body later. Still, he pulled Flynn's hair and begged for more.

"Goddamn, baby boy. You don't know," Flynn said as he nipped at Jake's neck. "It's been so fucking long since anyone has been inside me. I know we were meant to meet. I feel it."

Jake scratched at Flynn's skin, trying to get closer. He felt it too. "Daddy." The word came out sounding pained—like a plea. Jake couldn't stop. "What are you doing to my head? I want things I've never wanted." The words tumbled out without his permission. He bit his lip, holding back his confessions.

"I'm teaching you to live," Flynn said, making the world go quiet. Everything snapped into focus. He wanted to be taught. Guided. He needed someone to give him permission to be the person he wanted to be. It was okay. Jake never had to be ashamed as long as he was with Flynn.

Jake pulled Flynn's hair hard, forcing him to hold his stare. "Come for me, Daddy. I want your cum coating my skin."

Flynn's muscles hardened. A cry tore from his throat. Hot jets of cum poured out onto Jake's stomach and chest. Flynn's ass tried sucking Jake deeper. A blinding orgasm ripped from Jake, stealing his breath and stopping his heart. He scrambled for purchase as the world blew apart. The sounds coming from his throat were out of his control. When the storm passed, Jake's body turned to gelatin. He couldn't move as Flynn cleaned away their mess, caring for Jake the way he always did. When Flynn curled against his side, determined to cuddle, Jake stared at him in the dark, incapable of looking away. He was so in love. He wanted to say the words, but he wasn't that brave yet. Flynn hadn't pushed to hear them. The sudden and overwhelming need to know every detail of Flynn's life overcame Jake. This amazing man was his and Jake was free to do anything.

Flynn stroked him, rubbing every place he could reach. His silent, loving presence only fed Jake's need to fill the air with words. He broke. "Is it okay if I ask you a question?"

Flynn lightly stroked his fingertips back and forth across Jake's back. "Of course."

"When you were telling your story earlier, you

said William's last name was Thomson. The same as yours. Were you two married?"

"Aye. As soon as same-sex marriage was legalized in California in 2008, we got married. We'd talked about going to Catalonia for years to get married, but we knew it wouldn't be recognized here."

Jake expected it to hurt, hearing about Flynn with someone else. It was oddly moving. He felt like Flynn let him inside a space he didn't share with anyone else. Jake wanted more. "What was he like?"

"Hard," Flynn said to Jake's surprise. "William was gruff and unbending. He also worried more about other people than himself. You have to remember, I was the baby boy. He took care of everything and he took that job seriously. Then he died, and I didn't know who I was anymore. I was too old to be the person I'd been with William and too broken to want anything at all. So I disappeared into the lessons he taught me, losing myself while I searched for myself."

Jake fought the urge to squirm. He hated to ask, but he had to know. "Why me?" Too many times to count, he'd wanted to know why Flynn had broken every rule he'd set for himself for Jake. He'd toyed with the possibility that Flynn gave every man the same lines, making them feel special when he crossed a line he swore he never crossed.

"Why not you?"

Flynn's answer caught Jake off guard. He'd not expected to be put on the spot. "Because I'm me," he answered without thought. Once the door opened, confessions poured out. "There's nothing about me that stands out from the crowd. My brother has looks and charm. When we were kids, I always wanted to be like him. All he has to do is smile and people give him whatever he wants. Not that I'm wishing people would give me whatever I want, but life has been much easier for him. People don't notice people like me."

"I did."

A smile tugged at Jake's lips. "The night we met, we were alone in the front lounge of the Den of Payne for a good ten minutes and you didn't even know I was there until I spoke."

Flynn toyed with Jake's fingers. "That's only because you were hiding in a dark corner. Since the moment I caught sight of you, I haven't looked away. You're right that you're not your brother. Easton is like sweets. People rush for a piece but are usually left feeling empty and hating themselves." Jake wanted to defend his brother, but it was an apt description. "There's nothing wrong with that," Flynn added, soothing Jake's conscience. "There are people out there for him, guys who are looking for someone to show to their friends. You are the main course."

Jake snorted. "Thanks."

"You're welcome," Flynn said, refusing to let Jake brush off his words. "Because it was a compliment. You're what men look forward to at the end of the day. The one they're not ashamed for anyone to know about." Flynn lured Jake in, urging Jake to lean closer. "You're the sexy meal. The one people take pictures of to post on social media and brag how satisfying it tasted so all their friends are jealous." Jake blushed. Flynn could turn anything sexual. "People can live without sweets," Flynn said, urging Jake's lips to his. "I can't survive without you."

Well, damn. Jake believed him. As much as Jake realized he should've known Flynn's answer would be mind blowing, he hadn't known a thing. Even he saw his own appeal after that one. One day, he might not be so blown away by everything Flynn did. That day wasn't today.

FOUR

JAKE: *I love you.*

Flynn: *Wait. This isn't fair. I told you in person. Why do I get it in a text?*

Jake: *You know I'm not good at a lot of things. This is one of those things.*

Flynn: *You've gotten the first one out of the way. Now come out of the bathroom and tell me to my face.*

Jake: *I'm hiding in here until the embarrassment passes.*

Flynn: *Oi. <— that's a Scot's groan if you didn't know it.*

Jake: *I know. I heard your text.*

FLYNN: *DO YOU NEED ANYTHING FROM THE STORE?*

Jake: *Can I get a new back? This one is killing me. How did you do all this by yourself? How long did you plan to keep it up alone before telling me? This is a lot of freaking work.*

Flynn: *I'll be there to fix your back soon.*

Jake: *Okay. I'll wait. ILY.*

Flynn: *Goddamn. I hate that. Tell me you love me the right way.*

Jake: *I love you.*

Flynn: *Good boy.*

MOM: *CALL ME.*

FLYNN: *THE SIGN GUYS FINALLY SHOWED UP.*

Jake: *Thank God. I thought for sure we'd be opening tomorrow with no sign.*

Flynn: *Oh, I'm about to make them regret being late.*

Jake: *Damn. I wish I was there to see you in alpha mode. So hot.*

Flynn: *I'm always in alpha mode. Enjoy lunch*

with your brother. That way he doesn't show up here. That was a joke.

Jake: *I know, but really, he doesn't need to start showing up at the store.*

Flynn: *Damn, I love you.*

Jake: *I love you too. Now give the sign guys hell.*

Dad: *Stop ignoring your mother.*

Easton: *Did you give Mom and Dad your new number yet? They're blowing up my phone.*

Jake: *No, and if you give it to them, I'll never forgive you.*

Easton: *Sigh. Just tell them you'll do what you want and hang up. That's what I do.*

Jake: *Don't. You. Dare. I love you.*

Easton: *Fine. I love you too. You owe me lunch.*

The struggle was real today. Flynn couldn't keep his hands to himself. There was plenty of room behind the counter for Jake and him. Flynn couldn't stop invading the man's space. Jake's round ass was too tempting. Each time they had a break between customers, Flynn found his body molded against Jake's back under the guise of reaching past him. Jake made a tiny humming sound every time it happened. Flynn wanted more.

The shop had only been open a week. Business had been steady, and they'd blown away Flynn's income predictions. He wasn't worried about the money. Flynn needed Jake to see they could succeed. In the four months they'd spent working side by side, getting the store ready to open, Jake had slowly come out of his shell. The more Flynn told Jake he loved him, the more Jake smiled. Flynn savored every ounce of happiness he saw inside Jake. As far as he knew, Jake hadn't spoken to his parents at all. He'd only spoken about them in passing. His mom had lost her race for governor. Jake had mentioned it like he'd been giving Flynn the daily weather report. Flynn didn't push. When he'd walked away from his family years ago, he hadn't wanted to talk about it either. Anytime William brought up the topic, Flynn would kiss him. Some things cut too deep. Being born to parents ashamed of everything he did was one of those things.

"You're staring at me an awful lot today," Jake said, flashing him a knowing smile. "Are you plotting against me?"

Flynn swept his gaze down Jake's body, molesting him with his eyes. "Plotting ways to be pressed against you. Grinding against you. Making lots of friction. Dragging cries from your tired throat."

Jake's eyes flashed with a combination of heat and humor. He leaned against the register and returned Flynn's blatant eye fucking. It was so at odds with Jake's personality that Flynn was forced to lock his knees against a wave of lust. "You should—" The bell above the door jingled, cutting Jake off. They glanced toward the front. A man in an expensive business suit headed their way. His face was set in a hard line. His green eyes flashed annoyance—like their existence inconvenienced him. "Dad?"

Flynn's gaze swung Jake's way and back toward Jake's father. Damn. So this was Jim Woods. He looked like a man who berated his children. Hell, he looked like a man who berated baristas, his secretary, the weather for not cooperating ... everything.

His cold gaze slid Flynn's way. "Please excuse us."

Flynn didn't say no, but he also didn't budge. Jim gave him a sharp nod. "Very well." He focused on Jake, pinning him in place with his obvious disapproval. "Your brother told me where to find you."

"I wasn't hiding." Jake didn't sound defiant; merely resigned.

"A claim that's invalidated by your refusal to answer your phone," Jim said dryly as he took off his jacket and set it on the counter as if he expected it would take some time to get down his list of disappointments.

"Actually, I changed my number."

Flynn bit his bottom lip to hide his smile. Jake wasn't being rude. He sounded tired, but damn, Flynn loved watching him stand his ground.

"That's neither here nor there," Jim said, swiping his hand through the air. "I don't know what the hell is going on, but we made a deal. Four months of not being at Green's is long past the time you should've passed your bar exam. I'll call tomorrow and get the test scheduled for you."

Flynn fought the urge to interject. He couldn't do this for Jake. Plus, it was entirely possible Jake wouldn't choose him. This was the man's father. Jake shouldn't have to choose between Flynn and his family. Flynn wasn't the one drawing the line in the sand. But now he completely understood why William had always felt like he'd stolen Flynn from his family. Flynn was feeling that now. If Jake stuck with this store, his parents would not let it stand without ultimatums. They were too much like Flynn's parents had been. Too stubborn to see they would lose their son if they stayed this path.

Jake's shoulder lifted in a half shrug and fell as he visibly sucked in a deep breath. Flynn's heart cracked. They were hurting Jake by putting him in this position. Flynn hated this. "No."

Flynn blinked. So too did Jake's father.

"Excuse me?" The deadly note to Jim's tone warned his wrath would soon follow if Jake didn't take it back.

Jake nodded. Flynn got the feeling the move was for himself and no one else. "No. This place is the dream I had for myself before law school was pushed on me. I'm not happy on that career path. So, no. I won't be doing that."

Rage hardened Jim's features, oddly transforming him into a good-looking man. Jake favored him quite a bit. "After we spent a quarter of a million dollars on your education, your happiness doesn't compute. Law was your mother's path and mine. Now it's yours. You will fall in line with this."

Flynn could feel Jake's resolve cracking. He wasn't used to disobeying. Jake was grown and could choose his way but knowing that and doing it were two different things.

Even though he knew he'd regret it, Flynn spoke up. "If the cost of Jake's education is the issue, I'll repay you Jake's tuition costs."

Jake dropped his chin and stared at his shoes. Flynn could tell he was smiling by the curve of his cheek. In that moment, Flynn didn't care what his interference cost if it meant he made Jake smile in the worst of circumstances.

Jim's gaze cut Flynn's way. His features screamed outrage. "It's not about the money. It's the principles of upholding tradition. Jake was born into privilege he needs to respect. He—"

"What about Easton?" Jake asked, cutting off his father's building tirade.

Flynn was hard pressed to decide which of them was more surprised by Jake's interruption—Jim or Flynn. Jake might hate the life his parents chose for him, but he never, ever dragged Easton into things. Jake loved Easton—faults and all. It was possible Jake was the only one who still thought—one day—Easton would shock the world and become the person Jake saw. Personally, Flynn thought Easton would still pretend he was sixteen at sixty.

"What about your brother?" Jim snapped.

One of Jake's shoulders lifted in a half shrug again. "Why haven't you expected him to uphold the tradition and respect for the privilege he enjoys?"

A huge grin spread across Jim's face. He grabbed his side as he barked out a laugh. "Are you being serious? It's Easton. He probably doesn't know the difference between a quarter and a dime. No one would trust him to represent them in court."

Jake's expression underwent a subtle change. To anyone else, it might've seemed he wasn't affected by Jim's claim. Flynn saw the flash in his eyes. He understood what Jim did not. Jim had fucked up by talking badly about Easton. Jake would never budge now. The gauntlet had been thrown down.

"I'm not talking about becoming a lawyer. He has other talents. You spent two hundred and fifty thousand dollars on my education. Why not spend fifty thousand investing in his cake shop?"

Jim still hadn't realized the dangerous path he treaded. He snorted. "A cake shop? Are you fucking playing with me? What is it with you boys? A bookstore. A bake shop. It's like neither of you have an ounce of realism. I thought you—at the very least —understood that you have to work for a living. We don't bake cakes, sell trashy novels, and expect the money will roll in while we play. That's not this family's ideals. Be fucking real, Jacob. You're an adult. Easton will find some rich old man with one foot in the grave and another on a banana peel and he'll be set for life. Charm is his gift. Good sense is yours. Use your head."

"If I could interject," Flynn said, hoping to save Jim from totally alienating his son.

"Who are you anyhow?" Jim snapped, losing the facade of civility.

"A rich old man," Flynn spat as his anger spiked.

"With no banana peel in sight," Jake said, bursting into laughter. He covered his mouth, trying to stifle the sound.

Flynn smiled. He loved this man so much. No one could wipe away his temper in an instant the way Jake could. "Not that old, brat." For a second, they stared at each other smiling, sharing a moment.

"Uh huh," Jim said, ruining the mood. He gathered his jacket. "Next week. Bar exam. I'll pull some strings and make sure it happens. Be there."

Jake shook his head. "Don't call in any favors on my account. I won't be going. This is my job now and

I love it. I hope you can come to terms with this and love me despite your disappointment. If not," Jake shrugged, "it's not like I've ever felt loved by you anyhow, so no loss."

Flynn dropped his gaze to his shoes. He felt the loss, even if Jake didn't. Flynn already knew what it was like to walk away from the only parents he'd ever have and have no choice but to live with that decision. He didn't regret choosing William. Flynn hated them for not choosing their son. Now, here he was, witnessing the same sin. Jim and Patricia Woods were such fools.

An ugly snort left Jim as he draped his jacket over his arm. "Leave the dramatics to Easton. It's beneath you. Your mother will let you know when your test is scheduled."

Jake tossed a glance Flynn's way. He shook his head, as if to say he was done trying. Flynn held his silence until they were alone. The moment Jim disappeared from sight, Flynn tugged Jake into his arms. He pressed his lips to Jake's temple.

"Tell me what you need." He would do anything Jake asked.

"I have everything."

"Oh my gosh. Look at this place. It's amazing." At Easton's sudden appearance, Flynn ducked behind the counter before he was spotted. "Was that Dad I saw pulling from the lot?"

Flynn rolled his eyes. Easton had probably hidden in his car until the danger of seeing his father passed.

"Easton. Hey, sweetie. What brings you by?"

Flynn dropped onto his ass, sitting at Jake's feet on the floor.

If Easton noticed Flynn's defection, he didn't point it out. "Can I borrow your kitchen?"

"Of course. Why do you need my kitchen?" The way Jake agreed before asking any questions was telling. There was nothing Jake wouldn't do for the big brother who acted like he was younger.

"You won't believe it. I've had ten cake orders."

Flynn had no idea what was going on, but Jake was smiling, and Flynn couldn't look away.

"That's amazing. At this rate, you won't have to wait long to have your shop."

"I wish I didn't have to wait, but you're the only one who thinks I can do this, and I don't have anyone backing me like you do. This place looks fantastic, by the way. Maybe your secret benefactor could back me too," Easton said with a laugh.

Secret? Flynn stared at Jake so hard, there was no way his baby boy didn't feel his disapproval.

"Thanks. Flynn put most of the work in."

At the mention of his name, Flynn's irritation dimmed somewhat.

"When will I meet this Flynn anyhow?"

At Easton's question, Jake's chin dropped a hair as if he fought the urge to look directly at Flynn's hiding spot. "I guess whenever you're both in the same place at the same time."

Flynn fought back a chuckle. Easton wasn't Flynn's favorite person. He'd tried breaking up Kato and Brad. Flynn didn't exactly want to hang out with a troublemaker.

"Set up a place and time. I'll be there."

At Easton's chipper suggestion, Flynn swallowed a groan. Jake chuckled like he felt Flynn's discomfort. Flynn stared up the line of Jake's body. He was gorgeous from every angle. Not to mention, there was something about his happiness that made Flynn proud. When it came to Jake, Flynn became the caveman needing to provide happiness. He massaged Jake's calf. Jake's smile hitched up a notch. Flynn found his hand moving higher. He brushed his fingers up Jake's inner thigh. Jake shuffled closer. Flynn blocked out everything except the man beneath his hand. Sometimes, at the strangest of times, it would hit Flynn how funny life was. How every decision—big or small—steered people toward exactly where they should be. Never in a million years had Flynn expected to open a bookstore, or that he'd one day take on the same role William had played for him. He equally never expected to want the position. At one time, he'd been the baby boy looking for a safe place to be himself. Maybe he still was searching for a space to be free. After all, Flynn reveled in their unique relationship. He adored the way Jake opened himself, exposing his true face for only Flynn to see. Jake trusted Flynn in a way he didn't trust anyone else. It was beautiful. They were beautiful.

Flynn pressed his lips to Jake's thigh and inhaled. He swore Jake's essence filled his lungs. Jake's fingers swiped through Flynn's hair. Flynn wrapped his arms around Jake's legs and hugged him. With his cheek pressed to Jake's thigh and his eyes closed, Flynn held on. No one had showed Jake any real affection before Flynn. That was one thing Flynn knew for certain from Jake's mannerisms. The way he soaked up Flynn's attention and shyly touched Flynn in return said a lot about how little he'd been hugged and kissed as a child. Flynn couldn't get enough of being the one person who got to wrap Jake in his embrace.

"Flynn?"

Flynn tilted his chin up and met Jake's stare. It seemed Easton had left while Flynn had been engrossed in loving Jake.

Jake chewed his bottom lip as he stared down at Flynn. Flynn could see him working up the courage to give his thoughts a voice. He patiently waited. Jake had his attention as long as he needed it. A loud breath left Jake as he released his bottom lip. "You're amazing." A blush touched Jake's cheeks like he was slightly horrified by exposing his heart. Jake was strong, though. He didn't stop. "Being with you is the best part of my life."

Flynn set his chin on Jake's thigh and let a wicked smile grow. "Does that mean I can keep you tonight? You know you don't want to go home to that kitchen Easton won't clean." He squeezed Jake's ass. "There are other benefits too."

Heat filled Jake's eyes. "You don't have to bribe me. There's nothing I would rather do than be with you."

It was only a half hour from closing. Flynn didn't have that much patience. "It's slowed down to almost dead already today. We should lock up early." He massaged Jake's cock through his clothes. "Or you could risk it and I could blow you right now."

Jake didn't budge. Hunger twisted Flynn's gut. Like him, Jake was sexual to his core. Flynn slowly reached for Jake's zipper. He wanted to give him time to blink. Jake didn't back down. Flynn's lust hit a new height. Although Jake didn't see it, he was fearless. Flynn planned to suck his dick and fuck him right here, where anyone who walked in might catch them. For now, no one could see Flynn in his hiding spot, but it wouldn't be long before they couldn't hide their act.

"Tell me what you want, baby boy."

Jake didn't shy away or stammer. "I want my cock in your mouth until I blow. Then, I want you to fuck me right here, where anyone might catch us."

Goddamn. Who was he to deny his baby boy? Still, he hesitated after getting to his knees and setting Jake's erection free. He waited for the magic words.

Jake caressed his jaw before gently urging Flynn's mouth to his waiting cock. "Please, Daddy?"

Flynn's eyes fell closed at the plea. He kissed Jake's crown before circling it with his tongue. A noise came from deep in Jake's chest. Flynn sucked the tip of Jake's cock, teasing him. Jake's flushed face and crazed eyes drove Flynn insane. He massaged his own dick through his jeans, trying to alleviate some of the pressure. Jake was too tempting. Flynn loved the way Jake's cock felt on his tongue. The way it filled his throat. He lost track of everything—time and space. Flynn forgot anyone could catch them at any moment. He feasted. He sucked and licked, enjoying the moment and the noises Jake made. The inside of Flynn's underwear was soaked. He was so damn aroused, it was painful. Flynn bobbed on Jake's dick and put every ounce of skill he possessed in pleasing his man. Without realizing it, Flynn had Jake's pants around his ankles in his fight to explore every place he could reach.

"Yes, Daddy. I'm so close. Your mouth is so perfect."

Flynn sucked harder at the praise. A sound came from Jake like he was drowning. He clung to the edge of the counter and fucked Flynn's mouth. His hips rolled. Jake abused Flynn's throat. Flynn savored every second. He felt Jake tense. A single heartbeat sounded in Flynn's ears. Cum flooded his mouth and a cry ripped through the air. Flynn swallowed. Cum ran down his chin, dripping onto the floor. Flynn sucked and swallowed until there was nothing left. He swiped his chin on his shoulder as he came to his feet. Flynn was rougher than he intended when he grabbed the back of Jake's neck and hauled him forward. His mouth slammed down on Jake's with enough force he tasted blood. Jake sucked Flynn's tongue as if he needed the taste of his own juice. Everything Jake did made Flynn horny as fuck.

"Don't move," Flynn growled, shoving away and heading for the office. He ripped open the desk and found the lube and a condom. As he headed back to Jake, Flynn prayed they didn't get caught because he needed to be inside Jake more than he needed his next breath. Jake stood where Flynn left him—bare assed and waiting. Flynn's cock tried climbing out his pants at the sight. He wasted no time freeing his erection and suiting up. His hands shook as he fumbled with the lube. An aggravated growl escaped him when it squirted out faster than anticipated in his impatience. It would be more mess to hide if a customer came in. The vision Jake presented wouldn't let Flynn slow. He bent Jake over the counter and set to work. Flynn didn't baby him. He impaled Jake with enough force he nearly lifted him from the floor. The madness wasn't appeased. Flynn fucked Jake. It wasn't sweet. The sound of Flynn's hips slapping Jake's ass cheeks bounced from the walls. Flynn felt like he'd die without Jake's tight ass pulling and sucking at his cock as hard as possible.

He wanted to climb beneath Jake's skin and live there for good. If he fucked him hard enough, maybe Jake would accept they were one.

Jake dropped his forehead to the counter.

Flynn slapped his ass. "Watch the door." Flynn couldn't stop there. "Does it turn you on, knowing someone might see? They could walk by, look in the window, and see me buried in this sexy ass to the hilt. Do you like the idea of someone watching this daddy fuck his baby boy?"

A loud moan escaped Jake. He didn't answer.

Flynn shifted positions, draping himself over Jake's back. He bit Jake's shoulder and fisted the man's dick. "Your kinks are safe with me," Flynn said, softening his tone. "It's okay to be slightly twisted. I love your naughty side. Does it make you hard to think of someone touching themselves while we fuck?"

"Yes."

It was the tiniest whimper of an answer, but it sounded like a cannon to Flynn's heart. He loved this closet kink. In the heat of passion, Jake would do anything. Their life together would never be cold.

Flynn kissed the spot he'd bitten. He slowly pumped inside Jake. "I think a trip back to the Den of Payne is in order. There's a room with two-way mirrors. You should see the crowds that gather, sitting in the dark. Some openly masturbating while others try to hide the way they touch themselves." Flynn swallowed as the pressure against his crown threatened to burst free. He wasn't ready. "I could cuff your hands above your head, and you'd be at my mercy while dozens watched. They'd stifle moans while I pull cries from your throat. You know I can make you beg for it." Jake whimpered. The sound nearly crippled Flynn. He sucked in a hiss. It sounded in his words as he kept up the narrative. "I could strap you to one of the swings with your legs spread just enough for the voyeurs to enjoy. We could take your favorite dick-sucking toy so you could come as much as you like while I torture your hole, stretching you with my dick and a dildo." Jake's cock was hard again in Flynn's hand. He could feel it pulsing. Flynn knew Jake could picture the scenario he painted. Sticky pre-cum dripped from Jake's dick, painting the floor. Flynn was barely clinging to his sanity. He massaged Jake's erection as he rocked inside Jake. "I don't share," Flynn said, hearing the growl in his voice. "But I'd let people watch as I claim what's mine. I'd let them fuck their fists and fingers while I take this perfect arse. Do you want it?"

"Yes," Jake whimpered, louder and more desperate this time. "Let them watch. Please, Daddy."

Jake's plea ripped an orgasm from Flynn with such power, one of his knees buckled. Flynn clung to Jake as wave after wave pulsed through him. He would never give this up. Jake was perfect. Together, they were everything he needed to survive. One day, he'd make that exhibitionist fantasy come true. For now, it was enough to know Jake was willing. Damn. He was a lucky bastard.

FIVE

IT WAS a little sad how hard it was for Jake to keep his hands to himself while Flynn tried unlocking the store. He always looked perfect with his thick hair combed back and styled. The red locks were so dark, his hair looked brown until Jake got close—like he was now. Flynn laughed while Jake held onto his back and kissed between his shoulder blades, making it as hard as possible for Flynn to do anything.

"Oh, hell," Flynn said with a sigh. "Do you have your key? I grabbed the wrong set."

Jake caught himself before he asked how many sets of keys he needed. He wasn't surprised he needed more than one. Flynn's house was huge. Not to mention, in the ten months they'd been together, Jake had only seen Flynn drive the same Chevy

Suburban each day, even though there were three other cars in his garage.

Jake kept one arm around Flynn's body as he dug the keys from his pocket. He purposely shifted closer, bumping Flynn's ass. A sexy chuckle rumbled from Flynn.

"You're making it hard for me to want to work today."

Jake brushed his lips across the back of Flynn's neck. "I hope that's not the only thing I'm making hard."

A groan escaped Flynn. "Damn, baby boy. You are such a temptation. If you understood exactly how much power you have over me, I'd be scared right now."

Jake rolled his eyes and unlocked the door. He didn't have any power over Flynn, but he liked hearing it. Plus, he was just in a great mood today. He had his dream job now and his fantasy man. Jake was currently running on three hours of sleep, but he'd spent those cradled against Flynn's chest. He also had only managed three hours because he'd spent the rest of the night exploring Flynn's body. No one had ever given him so much freedom while keeping him tied in knots.

Jake shoved through the door. He sighed. "It's

fine. I'll leave you in peace," Jake said in mock disappointment.

Flynn growled as he overcame Jake. He spun Jake in his arms and attacked his mouth, kissing him deep. He nipped at Jake's lips. "Wicked sprite."

Happiness overwhelmed Jake. Nothing could ruin this day. "Let's count in the register."

Flynn winked and walked away. Jake followed on his heels and watched it happen. Flynn moved like a man who knew how to please. Eyes always followed him everywhere he went. Jake never stopped being in awe that Flynn wanted him. He spent the rest of the day chewing his bottom lip and casting heated looks Flynn's way, wishing his life away so he could be back in bed with Flynn.

Hours passed in companionable silence. They worked side by side. Jake had found his version of heaven with Flynn. The bell above the door jingled. Jake tore his gaze away from the office door where Flynn had disappeared only minutes earlier and glanced toward the front. His breath left him. A young guy in a black leather jacket and jeans headed his way. His full lips were curled into a wicked smile. Sin bled from him as he crossed the room, holding Jake's stare. Jake stood frozen, waiting.

"I'm looking for my dad." He leaned over the

counter and dropped his gaze to Jake's shoes before slowly lifting his chin to meet Jake's stare. Jake swore he felt the guy's perusal like a physical touch as he lingered in all the right places. "But I'm thinking I found someone better."

To Jake's horror, his face exploded with fire. The way the boy's smile turned even wickeder didn't help matters. No doubt the guy was closer to Jake in age than Flynn, but he looked like a teenager and Jake felt like an old perv beneath the boy's heated stare—like he'd just been fucked in his clothes. By a teen. A sexy teen. A teen way more in touch with his kinky side than Jake would ever be. Goddamn.

"Stop molesting my man with your eyes 'fore I rip them from your head, Trace."

Jake's gaze jumped to Flynn as he appeared from inside the office. Guilt washed over him, even though he hadn't done anything wrong... possibly.

Trace released a loud and forlorn-sounding sigh as he straightened away from the counter. "Yes, Daddy."

At the use of that term directed at his man, even in a sarcastic tone, Jake's guilt turned to rage. Flynn was his. Maybe they hadn't exactly talked about being exclusive, but Flynn had quit his job and told Jake he loved him. If he was keeping an even younger man on the side, Jake would rip off his balls. For real, Flynn didn't know who he'd fucked with.

"No," Flynn said, keeping his tone soothing as he pointed at Jake and held his stare. "Donnae be looking at me like that." Goddamn bastard, breaking out the thick accent on Jake. Flynn shook his head. A self-deprecating smile touched his lips, as if his thoughts warred with his need to lecture. "Fuck me, but you are even sexy when jealous." He cleared his throat and squared his shoulders, visibly getting back to the heart of the matter. "Nonetheless, don't go thinking what you're thinking. I'm a lot of twisted things, but I'm no cheat." See? Exclusive. Just as Jake expected. Still. He refused to respond while he waited for an explanation. "He's really my son."

"Oh." For real, that one word popped out, then all thought ceased. Jake's brain came to an immediate halt in a way he'd never experienced before. Flynn had a son. Jake's gaze moved between them. Their eyes were an exact match. The boy's wicked smile that would magic the clothes from people's backs looked exactly like Flynn's. It all matched. Jake had questions. Surely he did, but no words came.

"I think you've broken his brain," Trace said out of the corner of his mouth. It was a cute move that would've charmed a smile from Jake under any other circumstances. Right now, he had nothing.

Trace reached over the counter and held out his hand. "I'm Trace."

Out of pure habit, Jake accepted his handshake.

Trace immediately brought Jake's hand to his lips. For the briefest moment, Jake felt that devilish grin against the back of his hand before Trace released him. "Don't be angry. I told Dad he shouldn't tell you about me right away. Being as how we're so close in age," Trace added with a wink. "I'd hate to steal you from underneath an old man."

Nope. Still nothing.

Trace's smile slipped a hair. "Really, most people don't want to take on someone else's kid, even though I'm nineteen and grown."

"You're not grown," Flynn growled, bringing Jake's gaze his way. He looked nervous—like Flynn expected Jake would run now.

Jake's throat loosened its grip on the lump choking him. He focused on Trace once more. "It's nice to meet you, Trace. I'm Jake."

"Yay. Good. Everything will be great. You'll see," Trace said, sounding excited. He focused on Flynn and held up a set of keys. "I accidentally took your keys this morning. Since mine are now missing, I'm assuming you ended up with them."

Flynn swapped sets with Trace and shoved them in his front pocket. "Thanks. I've been looking for those."

Trace dipped his chin. His wicked gaze swung back Jake's way. "I have to run but come by sometime. Have dinner. Get to know me." He eye-fucked Jake one more time. "You might enjoy it."

A loud, long sigh came from Flynn. It sounded like it pulled from his soul. "I'd lie and say I donnae know where he gets this, but the apple isn't far from the tree."

Trace winked and gave Jake a tiny finger wave before walking away. Jake watched him go. He wished he wasn't angry, but with every passing moment, the numbness disappeared and fury grew.

Jake turned away from Flynn and focused on the register. There was nothing for him to do there, but it was better than the alternative—tearing off Flynn's skin.

"You're angry."

Jake blinked at the machine in front of him. He fought the hot tears that pressed on the backs of his eyes. Some days, despite everything Flynn had done and said to the contrary, it felt like Jake would never mean anything to him. A son was a huge fucking deal, yet Flynn had never said a word. Jake cleared his throat. He would not give anyone the pleasure of seeing him break. "You lied to me. Maybe it was by omission, keeping secrets, or whatever, but it definitely feels like a lie."

To his surprise, Flynn was the one whose temper slipped. His hand slammed down on the bar. "I asked you to move in with me, to be a bigger piece of my life. You didn't want it." Jake's gaze jumped to Flynn's. There was so much hurt and open rejection written on Flynn's face. Jake had never suspected he'd wounded Flynn by not moving in with him. He'd thought he'd been doing the right thing. He'd thought Flynn had only offered out of kindness. Jake hadn't for one second believed Flynn had asked because he wanted Jake to move in. "You didn't want me," Flynn said, sounding desperate. "I didn't want to introduce my son to someone who thinks of me as temporary."

A woman appeared at the counter, snagging Jake's attention. "Excuse me. I don't know if you can help, but I'm looking for a book and I can't remember the name."

Flynn walked away. Jake tried not to watch it

happen. "Tell me what you can recall, and I'll try to help."

She smiled. "It's about a homeless teenage boy who gets taken in by this man." Jake tried to concentrate. Everything was a blur. He was so stunned and hurt that he couldn't even focus on the woman's features, much less her words. His gaze slid to where Flynn stood nearby, staring at a shelf with unfocused eyes. Jake's mind raced. He didn't really care Flynn had a son. That was a story he wanted to hear. He craved every memory and tale Flynn had to share. Even the ones that involved William. They'd shared a beautiful life together. William had shaped Flynn into the gorgeous soul Jake loved with every ounce of his being. Jake took a breath. Flynn really wanted Jake to live with him. Jake wanted more than that. He craved everything. All the times he'd stayed quiet when his heart screamed for more rose in Jake's chest. His skin itched. Too many times to count, Jake had held his tongue, missing out on the life he wanted to keep everyone else happy. Jake didn't want to do that anymore. Flynn had taught him better. Jake couldn't hold his tongue and hide his desire anymore. He needed all of Flynn.

"Excuse me," Jake said, cutting off the woman mid-sentence. "I just need to do something real quick. Give me a second." He walked away, uncaring of anything but Flynn. His heart pounded in his ears as he moved in Flynn's direction. His hand slid across Flynn's back with no real plan. Flynn turned. His amazing blue eyes looked sad and Jake fucking hated that. "I love you."

Flynn's mouth lifted in one corner, but none of the hurt left his eyes. "Same."

Jake's heart rate increased, making him lightheaded. "Will you marry me?" The moment the question left his lips, fear set in full force. "I want to live with you. I've always wanted that. It's just, I thought you offered out of sort of sense of charity or whatever. But I've wanted everything, a full life with you, since the moment I realized seeing your face made every shit thing that happened disappear. I just never thought you'd want me full-time." He couldn't stop the rambling. "We're so different. You are so put together and I'm just not. I'm not very good at showing emotion. But I love you and I want to get married and I'm good with you having a son and I'm happy with..." Jake trailed off mostly because he lost his breath. Flynn's bright smile also stole his thoughts. Jake kissed him. He didn't think about where they were or who watched. All Jake's thoughts were occupied by loving Flynn. He loved this man more than anything. If this bookstore failed or his parents never said they were proud of him, none of that mattered. This man was all that Jake cared about. He would not let him hurt or be disappointed. Jake would do anything to please him. Even if it meant putting his heart on the line and saying his dreams aloud. He wanted to marry Flynn. That was his biggest wish and scariest confession. He trusted Flynn with everything.

"Aye," Flynn said against Jake's lips. His arms tightened around Jake, squeezing the air from his lungs. "Help the lass find her book and we'll lock up so we can get married."

Excitement shot through Jake. "Are you serious? Today? You want to get married today?"

Flynn stroked Jake's jaw. "Aye. I'm not giving you time to change your mind. Plus, there's nothing I wouldn't do for my baby boy. You are my whole heart. I love the idea of giving you my last name."

With sore cheeks from smiling, Jake headed back for the counter. Heat flooded his face as he noticed the woman staring and smiling. "I'm sorry." Even Jake heard the horror in his voice. Public displays of affection were so out of his comfort zone, he didn't know where to start. "Tell me about this book again."

With a laugh, the woman swiped her hand

through the air. "Never mind. I'm good. Once I think of it, I'll be back. You should lock up behind me before anyone else shows up and slows you down. The county clerk's office closes at four." She headed for the door. Jake followed on her heels, trying to beat back his horror and hide his excitement. A girl who looked to be about fifteen tried coming in as the lady went out. The woman physically spun her in the opposite direction. "They're closed today, chickie."

Jake bit back a laugh as he turned the lock on the door. This was really happening. The world was conspiring for them. In a few short hours, he'd be married to the man he loved more than life. It couldn't be real. Jake turned and found Flynn staring at him with the same expression of awe that Jake felt to his soul. In that moment, Jake wasn't scared. More times than he could count, Jake had done things demanded of him that felt wrong on every level. Flynn wasn't one of those things. He was the one right thing Jake could claim. Jake had never been surer of anyone or anything in his life.

SIX

JAKE SWORE the sun shone brighter since marrying Flynn. They hadn't gotten married on the same day Jake asked only because the line was too long. It had turned out to be a blessing in disguise. Once they'd taken a breath, they both realized they each had a family member they wanted with them. So they scheduled an appointment for the next day, rounded up Trace and Easton, bought rings, and had the only wedding Jake ever dreamed of having—a marriage to a man of his choosing.

While leaned against the kitchen counter, Jake sipped his coffee and stared at Trace. If Trace noticed, he didn't let on. It was surreal as hell for Jake, realizing he was someone's step-father. Trace was only seven years younger than him. He was nineteen and grown. Trace was also larger than life. His personality was so huge and overwhelming, Jake lived in awe he'd managed to hide from Jake for nearly a year. Flynn's house was big, but not obnoxiously so. While it was true Flynn had spent more nights at Jake's than Jake had spent here, they'd still never crossed paths. The curiosity ate Jake alive.

"How did you manage to keep yourself hidden this whole time?"

Trace glanced Jake's way. His blue eyes that looked so much like Flynn's flashed with humor. "I can be very sneaky when my mind is set to it."

Flynn cleared the kitchen door just in time to hear Trace's claim. He ran his hand through the boy's hair, leaving it standing on end. "That he can. That is, when he's actually here," Flynn added as he crowded Jake against the counter. "Alright, sexy. Where have you been all my life?"

Heat filled Jake's cheeks at Flynn's playfulness. "Good morning."

A sexy hum escaped Flynn as he leaned in and stole a kiss. He leaned away before things turned too heated.

Trace stood, sipping his coffee and openly staring.

Jake blushed.

Trace smirked. He was definitely his father's son. "I don't actually live here," Trace said, going back to their earlier conversation, as if they hadn't been interrupted. "At least, not full-time."

Flynn poured himself a cup, joining the conversation. "Trace owns a nightclub in Aspen. He only sleeps here when he's in town."

"Wow. Nineteen and a club owner. You can't even buy alcohol yet. I'm impressed."

"Don't be," Trace said, waving off Jake's praise. "I'm only as good a businessman as my parents taught me to be."

"He helped out with paperwork—work orders, payroll, vendors, and whatnot back when the bar was open." Flynn sounded proud.

"Started working when I was twelve," Trace said, adding to the conversation. "Most kids I knew had to take out the trash. I had to know how much beer and liquor a bar would need to stay open on a busy weekend. Then, Dad died." Trace shrugged and didn't say more.

In an instant, Jake felt like an intruder, living in William's home. He'd been upset when he'd learned of Trace's existence, but not because he was William and Flynn's son. It had only been because he'd felt lied to. Once that passed, and he'd asked a few questions, learning about the journey of a gay couple and surrogacy in a time it might not have happened if William hadn't been rich, Jake had been fine with everything. This was the first time he'd truly felt out of place with Flynn.

Jake's gaze slid Flynn's way. He watched as Flynn doctored his coffee, oblivious to Jake's inner turmoil. Trace touched his arm, pulling Jake's attention back his way. Without a word, Trace took Jake's coffee cup from his hand and set the cup aside. Before Jake had time to guess at Trace's intentions, he found himself wrapped in Trace's arms. Trace squeezed until Jake couldn't breathe.

"I'm so glad my dad found you," Trace said against Jake's ear, keeping the words between them. "He needed you to come storming into his life."

The ache in Jake's cheeks made him realize how big his smile had become. It was truly a case of like father like son. Just as Flynn seemed to always know how to fix Jake, Trace was the same. "You have no idea how much I needed him." Jake couldn't have stopped the confession if he tried.

Trace placed a noisy and wet kiss on Jake's cheek, leaving Jake swiping at his face. "All right. Stop flirting," Trace said in a loud voice. "That's so unseemly of a step-parent. I'm pretty sure people go to jail for that."

Jake shook his head at Trace's antics. He looked to Flynn for help.

Flynn shrugged and sipped his coffee. "He's not wrong."

Without thought, Jake lightly punched Flynn in the stomach. The sexy chuckle that rolled from Flynn's lips, as he rubbed the spot he'd been hit, wiped away any embarrassment Jake felt over his actions. He never play fought with anyone. Being with Flynn was changing him.

"You two should get to work before the bookstore loses another day of business thanks to your inability to keep your hands to yourselves." Trace shooed them toward the door.

To Jake's surprise, Flynn didn't take charge. He let Trace push them out. When they climbed inside Flynn's Suburban, Jake realized why as he found himself attacked. Flynn kissed every place he could reach, leaving Jake breathless.

"You're very sexy this morning, Mr. Thomson."

Jake let Flynn's compliment wash over him. He wondered if he glowed from all the happiness. "I love it when you call me that."

Flynn whispered Jake's new name against his ear

a few more times as he caressed Jake. It might've gone on all day if Trace hadn't hit the button on his car alarm, startling them from the bubble where they'd disappeared.

Flynn groaned as he started the car. "I guess that was our cue to leave. He probably has someone coming over he doesn't want me to see."

Jake laughed as he buckled his seatbelt. "Why would he not want you to see them?"

"He's my son," Flynn said, keeping his gaze locked on his task. "No doubt, whoever he's with, you can guarantee I wouldn't approve."

Flynn's claim had Jake's mind churning. Considering all the things Flynn had done, he wondered who could possibly merit Flynn's disapproval. He didn't get to mull it over for long. The second they pulled into the parking lot of the bookstore, Jake spotted his mom waiting.

A groan rose in his throat. "Damn. First thing. This looks to be a great day."

Flynn didn't argue, which meant he agreed.

Jake slipped from the vehicle, already bitching and in denial.

"Mom. No. I already told Dad when he came by—"

"I don't give a shit about any of that," she said,

sounding terror-stricken as she rushed across the parking lot. At her panicked tone, Jake looked at her closer. Her hair was a mess, and she wasn't wearing makeup. She snagged him by the wrist and started for her car, practically dragging Jake across the lot and shocking him with her strength. "Your brother is in the hospital and apparently patients can refuse visitors, even if it's their parents. He won't refuse you."

At the news, Jake's reluctance disappeared, replaced with fear. "Oh my god. What happened?"

She didn't slow. "I don't know. We'll talk about it in the car."

Jake tossed a panicked look Flynn's way.

Flynn waved him away. "Go. I'll call Trace in to run the store today and come after you."

Reassured Flynn would take care of everything, Jake scurried to keep up with his mom. Once he was safely belted inside her BMV, Jake focused on his mom. Her hands were shaking. Jake wondered if he should offer to drive, but he wasn't exactly feeling steady either.

"What happened to Easton? Is he okay?"

Patricia shook her head. "I don't know. They won't let me see him. Easton wouldn't let me in the room. All I know is what the police told me when they came by the house." Her voice shook harder than her hands. She took a breath. "They found him in an alley behind some club downtown. He still had his wallet and phone. That's the only way they could identify him." She choked on the final words and tears spilled over her lashes. Jake's tongue refused to work. Chills ran through him, taking away the heat of the day. He fought the urge to demand she stop the car. Jake's stomach churned. He kept his gaze locked straight ahead. His thoughts whirled. What had happened to his brother? The drive passed in a blur. As his mother claimed, a nurse stopped her in the hallway, refusing her entrance into Easton's room. Despite the nightmare they were currently living in, Jake fought a small smile. It seemed, even in this horrible situation, Easton had maintained enough charm to cause these overworked nurses to take him under their wing and protect Easton's privacy.

"What's your name?" At the nurse's question, Jake's mind snapped into focus.

"Jake Thomson."

"Woods," Patricia snapped. "His name is Jake Woods."

Jake shrugged. He didn't have time for this right now. "Whatever."

The nurse didn't seem to care about their disagreement. She clicked around on the computer. "Here you are. Jake Thomson. Easton said it was okay for you to visit."

"Why does everyone keep calling you by that name?" Patricia snapped, obviously at her breaking point with Easton still not letting her into his room.

Jake headed for the Easton's door. "Because I got married," Jake said over his shoulder as he slipped inside the room and out of range of his mother's temper.

His steps faltered at the first sight of Easton. As the police claimed, he was unrecognizable, except for his eyes. Those were the same gorgeous green they'd always been. He focused on Jake. It was like there was no one there beneath the deep lacerations, scrapes, and bruises. Everything that made Easton, Easton was gone. Jake's throat swelled. Tears filled his eyes. Easton lifted the covers. Jake didn't hesitate to cross the room and crawl into the spot beside him. As children, they'd done this nightly. Even though Easton was only eighteen months older than him and normally behaved like the younger brother, Easton had been the monster killer. His bed had been free of nightmares, his closet free of beasts, and he'd kept Jake safe from the dark. Jake had thought Easton was the strongest person in the world. It gutted him to see Easton defeated. Jake wrapped his arms around Easton and held on. It was back to being them against the world, except it was Jake's turn to be strong and keep away the monsters.

———

WITH JAKE'S PHONE IN HIS BACK POCKET, FROM where he forgot it in the front seat, Flynn headed for the hospital. He'd been forced to call Brad, who called Jim just find out where Easton was at and which room. Jim had been a bit more forthcoming with Brad than Patricia had been with Jake in her panic. Thanks to Jim's everlasting hope Brad would still join the Woods family someday, Flynn knew the whole story. Well, he knew as much as the police. Easton had been attacked while walking to his car after leaving his usual nightclub. Flynn tried to breathe. It was his worst fear for Trace. His son was so independent. Like Easton, Trace thought he was safe alone at night. Easton had been wrong. Flynn prayed Trace never met the same fate. Easton hadn't been robbed. Money had nothing to do with it. Three men, gang mentality, and power over someone weaker had fueled the situation. Easton would live, but he probably wouldn't want to for a long time. Flynn felt sick for him, but his heart bled for Jake. His baby boy would bleed in silence over this one. As much as he tried to hide it, because he feared Easton didn't really want it, Jake loved his brother. When it came to Easton, Jake hoped and dreamed like a parent, praying their child would eventually find their way. All Flynn could do was be there for Jake. He hadn't felt this helpless in a long time.

Before Flynn made it to Easton's room, he spotted Patricia pacing outside the door. At his approach, a tiny blonde nurse cut him off. "May I have your name?"

"Flynn Thomson."

At his name, Patricia moved closer. "I take it you're my new son-in-law."

"You're on the list, Mr. Thomson."

Flynn had no idea what that meant, but he gave the nurse a sharp nod and faced off against the woman who would no doubt hate him as much as his own mother did. "I wasn't aware you'd heard, but yes."

Her chest expanded and she crossed her arms as if to protect her heart. "It seems everyone is allowed to visit my son but me." She looked a complete wreck. Flynn's heart went out to her against his better judgment.

He set his hand on her elbow and steered her toward the room. "Let's go."

"She's not allowed in there," the nurse called at his back.

Flynn glanced back. "We won't bother him. She just needs to set eyes on him."

"I'm sorry," she said, not backing down. "We have rules."

Flynn didn't give an inch either. "What would you do if it was your child?"

The woman deflated. Flynn didn't give her time to argue again. He rushed Patricia to the door. It was possible the nurse would call security or whatever. He felt a little guilty. No doubt the nurse was already overworked without having to babysit Easton's door, but if it were Trace, they wouldn't keep Flynn out. Overbearing or not, Patricia needed to see Easton was alive. They slipped inside the room, stopping just inside the doorway. Jake and Easton seemed to be in their own world. On their sides, facing one another, Easton toyed with Jake's fingers and talked a mile a minute like a child. Patricia covered her mouth and leaned against the wall, hiding behind the curtain that kept the room private even with the door open. Her eyes swam with tears. Flynn got it. Easton didn't look like Easton. He had a bad feeling he wouldn't ever look the same again. Flynn silently tugged the curtain all the way closed, keeping them hidden so they wouldn't break up the brothers' conversation. He left a small crack so he could watch them. It always amazed him Jake didn't realize his strength. Flynn saw it. He was proud Jake was his.

"I have a bone to pick with you."

"Hit me with it," Jake said, sounding like he was the older brother humoring his baby brother. That was how the pair were. Flynn strained to hear every word.

"You should've had a wedding. It was your day. You should've had flowers and I could've made your cake. Oh, and I could've worn a white tux and tried to upstage you."

Jake snorted. "You don't have to try. You always upstage me. It's just a lucky thing Marcus has you locked down. Otherwise, I'd really feel like the ugly duckling at this imaginary wedding."

A beat of silence followed Jake's claim. When Easton finally responded, his happiness sounded forced. "Marcus called and dumped me about an hour ago. It seems I'm not that big of a prize now, but that doesn't matter. Old news. You're not an ugly duckling and you should've had a big day."

Jake looked like he choked on his rage, but he let Easton steer the conversation. "No one would've come," he said, visibly trying to hang on to a careless tone.

Flynn's eyes fell closed. Jake's pain was his. Anything that happened to Jake happened to Flynn. In that moment, Flynn saw the real Easton. He understood why Jake never gave up on him. Easton wasn't shallow. Not really. And Easton loved Jake. That was a position Flynn had to respect.

Easton refused to back down from believing Jake deserved the best. "For you, Mom and Dad would've been there, if you'd asked."

"It's sweet that you think so," Jake said, sounding sad. Flynn found himself watching Patricia, wondering how she felt about this conversation. She stared back at him in silence.

"They would have for you," Easton pressed. "I'm the throwaway child. But if you ever really stood up for yourself, they'd accept your choices."

"What do you mean you're the throwaway child?" Jake asked rather than continuing to argue his point.

"I didn't turn out how they wanted, so they

shrugged, tossed me to the side, and concentrated on you." Easton didn't sound upset, merely like he stated the facts. "You're the smart and dependable child."

Flynn's gaze slid back Jake's way. Jake flattened Easton's hand against his chest, holding Easton's palm against his heart—like he couldn't touch Easton anywhere else without hurting him. "Listen to me. You are *not* the throwaway child. You're my brother. I love you. You're irreplaceable."

Silence dragged on for a full minute before Easton responded, "You're the only person who ever tells me they love me and means it."

Jake's chest expanded and his breath came out sounding shaky. "Before Flynn, no one ever told me they loved me but you, period. You can't scare me like this again."

Patricia walked away. Flynn tore his gaze away from the pair and went after her.

"Whoa. Where do you think you're going, lady? You cannie leave with your sons like that," Flynn said, incapable of watching his accent in his irritation.

Patricia turned and met his stare. She looked more like Jake than he'd ever noticed in that moment. He'd seen this closed-off version of Jake too many times to count. Jake had learned this hiding method at his mother's feet whether he realized it or not. "My boys are better off without me. They have each other."

"You're a right fool if that's what you're thinking. I know. My parents pulled the same stupid shite when I was nineteen and we never spoke again. I moved to the States and they passed without n'er an apology and I'll never forgive it. It's not too late for you figure out that your sons may not be the people you dreamed they'd be, but they're still yours. I don't know Easton that well, but if Jake loves him the way he does, then there's got to be something great about him. And I know fer a fact that Jake turned out beautifully. If you spend the rest of your life thinking everyone has to be just like you or they're no count, then you deserve to be alone."

Patricia puffed up slightly. "Don't take it personally, but I don't need advice from someone who has no idea what it's to like to raise a child. You have no idea what it's like to sacrifice and plan for them to have the best of everything."

Flynn's eyebrows tried hitting his hairline. "Actually, I have a nineteen-year-old son. Congrats, you're a grammie." Without another word, Flynn walked away. His husband needed him right now.

He'd done all he could for someone who didn't want to change. Unlike her, he was welcome to visit, and Jake needed him.

Jake met Flynn's gaze as he came through the door. He pressed a finger to his lips and nodded Easton's way. It seemed Easton had finally talked himself to sleep. Flynn quietly eased down in a nearby chair, willing to stay as long as Jake needed. Up close, Easton looked even worse than Flynn first realized. Some of his cuts didn't look as if they'd been caused by a beating. They appeared closer to knife wounds. Easton wouldn't walk away from this unscarred. It didn't seem fair for the boy to look on the outside how he was on the inside. Easton and Jake had endured enough simply surviving their parents.

Flynn got comfortable. Two hours passed before Jake kissed Easton and whispered he was leaving. Easton woke enough to promise to call if he needed anything. It was obvious he had some painkillers in him by the way he fought and lost the battle with sleep. Jake looked battle-weary. Flynn kept his arm locked around Jake's waist all the way to the car. He took care of everything, buckling Jake's seat belt and ensuring he was cared for all the way home.

Jake's silence was terrifying. Once they were

home, he followed Flynn to the door with his head down. Panic started setting in. Flynn wasn't sure how to help. As Flynn unlocked the front door, Jake's arms encircled him. Flynn held still as Jake pressed his forehead to Flynn's shoulder.

"Daddy."

The hurt in Jake's voice nearly buckled Flynn's knees. He needed to fix everything. "Tell me, baby boy."

"I need you."

That was all it took to put Flynn in his place. He had everything Jake needed. Flynn pushed through the door, holding Jake's hand. He kicked off his shoes and headed straight for the recliner. Flynn pulled Jake into his lap and kicked out the footstool with Jake cradled against his chest. Jake buried his face in the crook of Flynn's neck. They sat in silence with Flynn holding Jake for what could've been hours. Flynn lost track of time. Nothing mattered except lending Jake his strength. He waited for Jake to find his voice again.

Jake shifted slightly and kissed Flynn's neck, coming back to life a hair. "He didn't even cry."

"I'm not surprised," Flynn said, sticking with the honesty Jake needed. "He's taught himself not to bother. Your brother is a survivor. My guess is too many men have enjoyed watching him break. He's learned not to give anyone the pleasure."

"I feel so useless. I don't how to help."

Flynn wasn't sure telling Jake there was nothing he could do was the right answer, but really, there was nothing anyone could do. Easton would have to fix Easton. In the absolute worst moments of people's lives, they were truly alone with their worst enemy— the mind.

"We'll find a way," Flynn said instead so Jake would know—like all things—they would face it together.

Jake kissed his neck again. "I love you."

Flynn squeezed him. "I love you too." Silence fell between them again. Flynn found himself filling it, needing his baby's happiness back. "You know how you asked me why you? This is why." Jake leaned away just enough to meet Flynn's stare. He looked so trusting and Flynn couldn't breathe sometimes for loving him. "Because of this," Flynn repeated while holding Jake's gaze. "Every time I've ever tried comforting you, it was me who ended up getting better. Just be there for Easton. If you can touch my heart, you can heal anyone, because I stopped feeling anything years ago. I should've been the one asking why me. You shouldn't have even looked my way. I'll do anything you need me to do. We'll fix this together."

Jake sniffed. The sound shattered Flynn's heart. He couldn't let his baby boy cry. Flynn kissed him, wishing like hell kisses really healed everything. One way or another, Flynn swore. He'd find a way to be all Jake needed to get through anything life threw their way. Nothing bad would touch his man as long as Flynn lived, even if that meant taking care of Easton too.

SEVEN

THE KITCHEN WAS A HUGE MESS. It looked like a flour bomb had exploded. Jake stared at the mess, torn between horror and wonder. On one hand, Jake feared Flynn would soon put Easton out on his ass if he didn't rein in his glorious cake-baking techniques. On the other, Jake was fairly certain there was flour on the ceiling and that was impressive. In the center of it all, Easton stood smiling while Trace praised his skills and offered to marry him.

"Seriously. This is... I'm speechless."

Easton caught sight of Jake. His smile faltered. "Don't worry. I'll clean it up before Flynn sees."

"Fuck that," Trace said, going back for a bigger bite of the five-layer chocolate masterpiece Easton had created from the chaos. "We can hire someone to clean up after you. You just concentrate on making more miracles like this. It's all good."

Jake shook his head. It was hard to scold Easton when he looked so happy. Jake had noticed Trace was good for everyone's ego. He was easily the brightest star in every room, bringing light to everyone around. He'd been so good to Easton. Jake held his tongue.

Easton waved off Trace's offer. "I made the mess, I can clean it up. After all, once the bakery opens, I'll have to get used to cleaning. Don't forget to take this with you when you head back to Colorado," he said, motioning toward the rest of the cake. "Who knows, you might expand my business into new states."

"I'm going to be so fat and I don't care," Trace mumbled around a bite.

"Don't talk with your mouth full," Flynn fussed as he appeared at Jake's back.

"I'm going to clean this up," Easton said before Flynn could say anything.

Flynn glanced around, taking in the mess. His expression didn't change. "It's fine. We could always hire someone."

Trace beamed. "See? That's what I said."

Jake could see Easton's panic rising. Since he'd

left the hospital and moved in with them, Easton had changed. Anxiety and nightmares kept him on edge. Jake had never been more thankful for finding Flynn. His calm handling of everything from financially backing Easton's bakery to getting him set up with counseling had made all the difference. Easton was a handful under the best of circumstances, but Flynn never batted an eye.

Before Easton could fall into a full-blown panic attack, Flynn wiped it away. "Besides, they say all geniuses are messy."

Easton blushed and looked away. "I'm not a genius."

"Bullshit," Trace said, still talking with his mouth full.

Easton bit his bottom lip and dropped his gaze to the ground, something he did a lot, trying to hide his feelings as much as his new scars. "I'll do the cleaning. You've already done too much, and I can't cost you any more money."

"Oh, don't worry over the money," Flynn said, hauling Jake back against his chest and wrapping him in his embrace. A smile tugged at Jake's lips as Flynn placed several noisy kisses against his throat. "I'm getting paid. Your brother has been taking it out in trade with his sexual services."

Trace covered his ears. "No. Innocent ears. No."

Flynn's sexy chuckle had goosebumps rising on Jake's skin. Sometimes he thought he was the luckiest person alive. The sheer number of tiny events that had to happen in just the right order for him to meet Flynn was astounding. It was almost enough to make him believe in fate. Flynn growled against his throat, making Jake's smile grow. "You're so distracting. I almost forgot why I came in here. We have visitors waiting in the living room."

Flynn's claim piqued Jake's curiosity. "Visitors?" He couldn't imagine anyone who'd come to see them. "Isn't everyone already here?"

"I guess you'll never know if you keep standing here."

At Flynn's mysterious tone, Jake's eyebrows rose. He glanced Easton's way. Easton shrugged and took off his pink apron. Trace grabbed his plate, refusing to leave his cake behind as they headed for the living room as one big unit.

Jake's parents sat waiting on the couch, looking more human than he'd seen in a while. His mom's dark hair was pulled up into a ponytail, while his dad wore jeans. Jake and Easton both froze at the first sight of them. As far as Jake knew, Easton hadn't seen either one since before his attack and Jake had only sent the occasional text to his mom, updating her on Easton's health. He hadn't known his parents even knew where they were living now.

"Your hair is up," Easton said, breaking the silence.

The corners of Patricia's mouth turned up, and she touched her hair. "I didn't want to be bothered with it today."

"You're not wearing makeup either."

At Easton's observation, Jake looked closer at her. It was a big deal for their mom to not look completely put together. Appearances mattered to their parents. Looking successful was the first step to being successful, according to all the lectures they'd gotten growing up.

"I've decided to retire," Patricia said, surprising Jake further. "There's no need to impress an empty house."

Easton looked lost—like he'd exhausted all possible lines of conversation.

"Something smells good," Jim said brightly, as if everyone wasn't crowding the doorway and refusing to move farther into the room.

Jake decided to meet them halfway. It was obvious his parents were trying. He took Flynn's hand and moved to the leather loveseat across from them. "Easton has been baking this morning, working out the menu for his bakery."

Patricia's mouth opened, and she glanced between them, looking shocked. "You're opening a bakery?"

Easton nodded, but Trace was the one who took charge. "He's amazing. Everyone will be fighting to get some of this," he said, pointing his fork at the cake on his plate. "You should try it."

Patricia visibly floundered for a moment, casting a look around the room before coming to her feet. "I'd love to." Trace brightened, obviously ready to pour on the charm as Patricia crossed the room. "So I hear you're my new grandson," she said as Trace led her from the room.

Jake and Flynn exchanged a look. Flynn looked innocent, but Jake knew. Flynn had done this. Somehow, some way, Flynn had brought his parents around.

Jim cleared his throat. It was an uncomfortable sound. "Where's this bakery?"

At their father's question, Easton inched farther into the room. "Flynn is building onto the bookstore."

Jim's usual hard stare moved Flynn's way. He didn't look the way he usually looked. Jake's dad looked... normal—like a person. It was odd. Jake had never really thought about his parents as regular people. They had always been so unfeeling toward Easton and him, he hadn't been able to see them as just people. It was more than obvious they meant to try.

Flynn urged Jake closer, making room for Easton to sit next to Jake. It was a tight squeeze, while Jim had the whole couch to himself, but Easton always seemed to sit on top of Jake anymore. It was like Jake was his safe place. Flynn had accepted things with aplomb. He never stopped amazing Jake. While Easton told their dad his plans for their joint venture, Jake found himself staring at the man who had completely transformed his life. He wondered if Flynn realized how much larger than life he was. Jake couldn't fathom being so silently powerful—to change lives the way Flynn did. Jake's hand moved to his stomach without thought. All of this amazing and powerful human was his. It was humbling and hot. Jake couldn't wait until they were alone again. After he forced Flynn to tell him how he'd pulled off today's miracle, Jake planned on paying out those sexual favors Flynn had mentioned earlier. Everything about Flynn turned him on. Flynn's gaze moved his way. He smirked, as if he read Jake's mind.

Damn, Jake was the luckiest man in the world. He would never take it for granted. As long as he lived, Flynn would know he was loved, just as Flynn never let Jake forget.

FLYNN'S SON, TRACE, HAS INSPIRED A SPIN-OFF series. His book will be the first in my upcoming Sugar Babies series, *Kinky Baby*.

ALSO, KEEP AN EYE OUT FOR THE NEXT BOOK IN the Sugar Daddies series, *Sugar Sentry*.

ABOUT THE AUTHOR

Charity Parkerson is an award winning and multi-published author with several companies. Born with no filter from her brain to her mouth, she decided to take this odd quirk and insert it in her characters.

*Eight-time Readers' Favorite Award Winner
   *2015 Passionate Plume Award Finalist
   *2013 Reviewers' Choice Award Winner
   *2012 ARRA Finalist for Favorite Paranormal Romance
   *Five-time winner of The Mistress of the Darkpath

Connect with her online:

--Join my street team: facebook.com/TeamCharityParkerson
   --Sign up for my newsletter: http:// bit.ly/CharityNews

--Website: charityparkerson.com

--Facebook:

facebook.com/authorCharityParkerson

facebook.com/TheMenofSin

--Twitter: twitter.com/CharityParkerso